LETTERS FROM A SEDUCER

'Like her friend and admirer Clarice Lispector, Hilst was a passionate explorer of the sacred and the profane, the pure and the obscene'
BENJAMIN MOSER

'A joyfully wicked writer'
TLS

'Hilst wrote with the ink of melancholy, the quill of playfulness, and, above all, a human body—a woman's body'
VICTOR HERINGER, AUTHOR OF THE LOVE OF SINGULAR MEN

HILDA HILST (1930–2004) was born in Jaú, a small town in the state of São Paulo. She studied law at the University of São Paulo before dedicating herself to writing from 1954. She published novels, poetry and plays and won many prestigious literary prizes, gaining recognition as one of the most significant and controversial figures in Brazilian literature. She resided at the Casa do Sol, a large estate that served as an informal artists' retreat and which she shared with a rotating cast of friends, artists, lovers and dozens of dogs. *The Obscene Madame D* is also available from Pushkin Press.

JOHN KEENE is the author, co-author, and translator of a handful of books, including the poetry collection *Punks: New & Selected Poems*, which received the 2022 National Book Award for Poetry, and *Counternarratives*, which received an American Book Award, a Lannan Literary Award and a Windham-Campbell Prize for Fiction. A 2018 MacArthur Fellow, he is Distinguished Professor and serves as department chair at Rutgers University-Newark.

LETTERS FROM A SEDUCER

HILDA HILST

TRANSLATED FROM THE PORTUGUESE
BY JOHN KEENE

WITH AN INTRODUCTION
BY BRUNO CARVALHO

PUSHKIN PRESS CLASSICS

Pushkin Press
Somerset House, Strand
London WC2R 1LA

Original text © 2018 by Daniel Bilenky Mora Fuentes
Published in Brazil by Companhia das Letras, São Paulo

English translation © 2014 John Keene
Introduction © 2014 Bruno Carvalho

Letters from a Seducer was first published as *Cartas de um sedutor* by Editora Paulicéia in São Paulo in 1991

First published in English by A Bolha Editora and Nightboat Books in 2014

First published by Pushkin Press in 2025

ISBN 13: 978-1-80533-138-4

All rights reserved. No part of this publication may be reproduced, stored in a retrieval system or transmitted in any form or by any means, electronic, mechanical, photocopying, recording or otherwise, without prior permission in writing from Pushkin Press

Offset by Tetragon, London
Printed and bound in the United Kingdom by Clays Ltd, Elcograf S.p.A.

EU RP (for authorities only): eucomply OÜ, Pärnu mnt. 139b-14, 11317, Tallinn, Estonia, hello@eucompliancepartner.com, +33757690241

Pushkin Press is committed to a sustainable future for our business, our readers and our planet. This book is made from paper from forests that support responsible forestry.

www.pushkinpress.com

INTRODUCTION

Bruno Carvalho

Born in Jaú, a small town in the state of São Paulo, Hilda Hilst (1930-2004) went on to become one of Brazil's most prestigious authors. Despite numerous literary prizes and steady critical acclaim, her work remains controversial among readers of Portuguese, and largely unknown in the English-speaking world. This edition of *Letters from a Seducer*, in John Keene's superb translation, should leave no one indifferent. It follows *The Obscene Madame D*, the first book by Hilda Hilst to be published in English, also by Nightboat Books and A Bolha Editora. In tandem, they make available to a broader public one of the twentieth century's most provocative and versatile writers.

Hilda Hilst began to publish while still a law student at the University of São Paulo. Between 1950 and 1962, she authored seven poetry books, the last of which earned her São Paulo's Pen Club Award. In the mid-60s, Hilda moved to a house in the outskirts of Campinas, São Paulo. Known as the "Casa do Sol" (House of the Sun), it hosted a myriad of writers and artists during Hilda's lifetime, including the sculptor Dante Casarini, her husband of many years. The "Casa do Sol" now houses the Hilda Hilst Institute. During the late 1960s, she began to split time between the Campinas residence and the "Casa da Lua" (House of the Moon) in the Massaguaçu beach. She also expanded her literary pursuits, writing plays and prose fiction. In 1969 she received the Anchieta Theater Prize, and in 1970 published her first book of fiction. For the next three decades, Hilda Hilst would continue to publish both poetry and prose, while amassing prizes and seeing several of her works adapted to the stage.

Letters from a Seducer, first published in 1991, was the third in a tetralogy of what the author deemed "brilliant pornography," or "porno-chic." These works followed a period of intense experimentation in Brazilian literature. The country had emerged from a military dictatorship (1964-1985), and writers no longer had to contend with brutal government censorhip. The constraints of the market, however, remained. Hilda Hilst did not attempt to produce best-sellers with this series, but she was playing with the boundaries of readers' expectations. While *Letters from a Seducer* is by no means conventional, it is in many ways one of Hilda Hilst's most enjoyable and stimulating works.

The book is divided in three loosely connected parts. All of them are narrated by a male voice. In the first, recalling the libertine epistolary novel tradition, the depraved and wealthy Karl writes to his sister Cordélia. Karl's foil, the dispossessed writer Stamatius, who goes by Tiu, pens the four short stories that comprise the second part. The last section includes seven fragments that can be read both as semi-autonomous vignettes, and in dialogue with the rest of the text. Karl and Stamatius, who refer to each other in less than amicable terms, take delight in exploring taboos: incest, pedophilia, murder, cannibalism. Most of the homosexuality focuses on man-man acts, rather than the woman-woman sex that prevails in heteronormative male porn. Much of the sex, however, revolves around male-centric ideas of female phallic fixation, and certain passages even verge on parodies of Henry Miller's literature.

BRUNO CARVALHO

Hilda Hilst maintains a reputation as a difficult author, a writer's writer. Much of her more experimental prose, including other works from her "obscene" series, can seem hermetic and impenetrable. In *Letters from a Seducer*, literary references abound. Almost every page alludes to a major author: Marx, Camus, Foucault, Genet, D.H. Lawrence, Tolstoy, Joyce, Madame de Staël, Nietzsche. Critics have pointed out parallels to Kierkegaard's *Diary of a Seducer*, as well as the narrative's metalinguistic elements. This is also a reflection about writing itself, about the limits of language and literary pursuit. Its appeal, however, is not limited to a bookish reader's abilities to decipher intertextual puzzles. To the contrary, like most pornography, *Letters from a Seducer* concerns itself with gratification, albeit mostly not of the erotic sort. In this work, where the trappings of pleasure are so often brought to the fore, it is not difficult to find pleasure at every turn.

The opening sentence offers useful clues: "How to think about pleasure wrapped up in this crap?" Crap can refer to the body and to language. Emil Cioran's epigraph offers a potential answer: "Life is tolerable only by the degree of mystification that we endow it with." No toothless mouth or raggedy body remains immune to the incantations of Hilda Hilst's vigorous prose. In the first sentence of the Portuguese version, the word for pleasure is *gozo*. Variations are translated elsewhere as joy, desire, to come (ejaculate). Like the French *jouissance*, it denotes enjoyment as well as a sexual orgasm. *Gozar*, the verb, can also mean to mock, to ridicule. Combining all these dimensions, *Letters from a Seducer* straddles the lines between seriousness of purpose and irreverence, erudition and kitsch, grotesque and black humor, sublime and sordid.

This translation captures that richness. It preserves the ambivalences, the shifts in tone and the rhythms of the Portuguese without ever feeling like a translation. Even more remarkable, a cornucopia of erogenous lexicon has been transposed into an English that contains all of the original's exuberance. The profusion of sex-related anatomical terms reveals an author's plunge, with painstaking philological rigor, into vernacular traditions, regional dialects, and dictionaries. As befits a poet and playwright, Hilda Hilst had a keen ear, and *Letters from a Seducer* turns the vulgar into something brilliant. Several passages of the book almost beg to be read aloud.

At the "Casa do Sol," Hilda Hilst engaged in experiments with recording unoccupied radio frequencies, resulting in mysterious voices which she claimed to be from the dead. Metaphysical questions permeate her work. *Letters from a Seducer* might seem otherwise, but in many ways it synthesizes several of her facets. Even when plotless, it is theatrical. Even amid pornography, we have poetry. And among clamors of the flesh, there are palpitations of spirituality. As the narrative progresses, death, god and the beyond enter the fray. In "The Pornographic Imagination," Susan Sontag writes: "If within the last century art conceived as an autonomous activity has come to be invested with an unprecedented stature—the nearest thing to a sacramental human activity acknowledged by secular society—it is because one of the tasks art has assumed is making forays into and taking up positions on the frontiers of consciousness (often very dangerous to the artist as a person) and reporting back what's there."[1] In *Letters from a*

---

1 Susan Sontag, *Styles of Radical Will.* New York: Picador, 2002. Pg. 45.

Seducer, Hilda Hilst's lifelong experiments with alterity break new grounds. She makes forays onto the limits of ponographic imagination, and amplifies the fringes of human sexual desire.

Regardless of whether *Letters from a Seducer* should be considered pornography or metaphysics, class and politics are not absent. In Stamatius's preamble he comes across ten thrown out copies of *Das Kapital*, and offers an aside: "it seems to be out of fashion, I guess…)." Stamatius (Tiu) rejects bourgeois life in the name of literature, a commitment that his partner Eulália indulges with occasional impatience. The hedonistic Karl, on the other hand, refuses neither the privileges of wealth nor editorial compromise. He becomes a published writer, to Tiu's chagrin. In literary or sexual pursuit, after all, no one is exactly like anyone else. Our wants evolve, devolve, resolve in ways that are often not linear, or recognizable to ourselves. But lack, like death, is a sort of equalizer, and not accidentally, a constant theme in literature. Eros spares no one, and it seems to be Everyman's truism that we can't get no satisfaction.

Karl and Tiu alike seek fulfillment. But it is Tiu who articulates the potential of scatology as a great equalizing force in a world of difference: "if everyone were to remember what comes out of their butt, everyone would be more generous, show more solidarity." Hilda Hilst's *Letters from a Seducer* invites readers to discover these voices, and find earnest insight in unexpected places. Seducer comes from the Latin *seducere*, meaning "lead away, lead astray." The pages ahead are sure to do so.

Life is tolerable only
by the degree of mystification that we endow it with.

EMIL MICHAEL CIORAN

LETTERS FROM A SEDUCER

How to think about pleasure wrapped up in this crap? In mine. This discomfort of knowing myself raggedy and covered with sores, your hair growing long in the crotch, if you dare think about it, and then around the hair a stew of wounds, I do dare think about it I tell myself, my mouth toothless because of all the stress and strain and addiction, I dare think about it and they don't forgive that. Then I take hold of your pubes and your pussy, pound them, your cry is high, hard, a whip, a bone, there's debris all over the room, shards of that church over there in Caturré, the guy blew up everything in five minutes (was it me?), screamed, darkly: God? here, oh I only know about God when I enter the hairy mouth of the wild sugar apple, and soon after we heard the bang, the church exploding like jackfruit falling from the sky. I take hold of my mistress's pudenda, after I spit on the papers, those ones from six months ago and which every day I smooth out, fumble with, tear, soil. Don't you want to fuck, Tiu? aren't you a little tired of writing? I look at Eulália. She's tiny and plump. For a year now she's been accompanying me in the street. We ask for everything that you are going to throw in the trash, everything that isn't worth a dime anymore, and if there is any leftover food we still want it. The burlap sacks fill up, bric-a-brac books stones, then some people put rats and shit in the bag, what faces those rats had, my God, what injured little eyes those rats had, my God, we separated everything out right there: rats and shit here, books stones and bric-a-brac there. Never any food. We were busy all day long. Afterwards I washed off the books and began to read them. Eulália would do what she could to get some food. What readings! What people of the first order! What Tolstoy and philosophy they threw out is unbelievable.

Letters from a Seducer

I have my half-dozen copies of that masterpiece *The Death of Ivan Ilich* and the complete works of Kierkegaard. And among the bric-a-brac I got some special ones too: a 12th century foot of Christ, half the face of an 18th century Teresa Cepeda y Ahumada, a piece of St. Sebastian's thigh (with arrow and blood) from the 13th century, a stick of pink plastic, from this century, all twisted up as if it had been burned (I kept it in order not to forget... not to stick mine in one of those spontaneously combustible pieces...), two parrot feathers, the belly of a Buddha, three pieces of angel wings, six Bibles, and two hundred and ten copies of *Das Kapital*. (They threw a lot of this last one out, it seems to be out of fashion, I guess.)

We're going to fuck, yes we are, Eulália, very soon.

She laughs. She has excellent teeth (!) and doesn't care about my empty mouth. She knows that I lost them (the teeth) when I was trying to pay my mortgage. The mortgage for my house. Stress. It is pretty clear that I was unable to do it, I found myself without house without teeth without furniture and without my woman. But the catfish here is whole, firm as you'll find, the tongue also, and I go on licking Eulália's little dove, her sweet coil, and she cries out a high cry, hard, a whip, a bone. Afterwards I insert the pole. When I come I take a peek at the bounty. My bounty here inside. What I did not have. The one I lost. I lost so many words! They were beautiful, blond, I lost "Monogatari," all her mountainousness, her monkey-cat-gnome-like acts, I lost Lutécia, a pathetic woman but mine. She died soon after saying to me: I'll go get some pasteles for you only. She was run over. My Lutécia. The crushed pasteles still in her hand. My Lutécia. Never again.

She was on the plump side and tall. And what softness in the cleft of her bosom, her chasm, in her bush, in her ass. What a butt! I laid my face there and sometimes half tearful, half silly, said to those stuffed meats, if I had had a little pillow like yours, Lutécia, when I was a filthy, shabby kid, I would have been a poet. Then she turned: cry here in my pussy, big boy, paint the rose, go on. I wept and painted it. She moaned sad and long. Eternal Lutécia.

what're you thinking about?

about our lives, Eulália.

and it isn't good, Tiu?

if I could at least manage to write.

write about me, about my life before I happened to find you, about the beating Zeca gave me, about the disease he gave me, about my mother who died of pity for my father when he utterly destroyed his liver, about the baby I lost, Brazil ay!

yes I'll write, Eulália, I will write about your tobacco leaves, about my bat.

don't talk like that, baby, I just want to help.

She lies face down, cries a little, afterwards whimpers, that's when I pluck the parrot's feather, one of those with yellow-green plumes, and whistling the national anthem I'll trill her little ass, sliding the shaft in the hole, slowly stroke the slope of her buttcheeks and Eulália rises and draws hers back loose, so I'm heading into the woods, and leave the pulp for the nib, beautifully stuck right in there. I come thick thinking: I am a Brazilian writer, something of a macho, baby. Let's go.

Letters from a Seducer

I

CORDÉLIA, my sister, come out of your cloister.

The countryside ages women and cows.

Once again nourish your holes

With gentle swine-cresses, blunt poles

Or if it's pussies your tongue wants

I'll get you dozens: mature cunts

Youthful cunts, purple cunts

for your vile, repressed feelings.

You were once the sluttiest, the most celebrated.

Perhaps a lady for a few brief seconds.

But now I find myself furious because I suspect

you hooked that paternal cock

In your deep holes. You traitor. Shrew.

Beloved muse still. I ought to bust your ass.

You'll return soon enough to an impure life

For if there are cocks in the world and quarrels

About everything, ah, Palomita, come on...

Here awaits you a squalid shelter.

Letters from a Seducer

My most beloved sister: I would like to touch you. But if that's impossible, I would like for us to write each other once again and for you to forget that little sentimental ruse of mine (you know what I mean), that nonsense from your young lover in a moment of extreme lust: he licked my crack (delicious, inexperienced but warm little tongue). And afterwards he confessed it to you in a tearful and disjointed jumble. Nonsense. Irrelevancies. The blame (was there blame?) was not the boy's. You know about my tricks to achieve that regal pleasure. You also know how much we loved each other, you and me, how much I made you happy, you screamed, even cried when my dick hit that. Don't ignore how competent I was doing the impossible, so that you thought (when you were with me) that you were actually fucking our dear father. (Luck that, even up until now or as far as I'm aware, we haven't had.) And I recognize that you made an effort to get me to think about mother when I was sucking your beautiful breasts. But I confess, Cordélia, how could I think of mother if she left (with that jerk) when I was just ten years old, and our deranged father burned all her pictures, and left us only one picture, taken from a magazine, of Princess de Lamballe, according to him the face of mother. And you think that I could think about mother at the moment of screwing, after having read at ten years old about the French Revolution (that disgusting spectacle of bloody heads ears and dicks) and reassure myself that Princess de Lamballe had her head decapitated, threaded onto a pike and exhibited, disheveled, to the queen? There are other details that at the moment I prefer to omit. One has got to stay horny, sister. But returning to your breasts. Because you had beautiful ones, my dear. Your nipples dark, slightly sweet. What did you rub on those beautiful nipples? I can say what it was because I once saw you in front of the mirror smearing "rosy honey" on your tongue, and whenever I asked about the odd sweetness of your tongue and breasts, you would say: because it's My tongue and because they're My breasts and because you love Me, Karl. I loved you, yes. Your little ass also knew that rosy honey, however your vagina was a mixture of yellow star apples and loquats. I remembered this very instant that these two trees are here at our orchard. What complicated alchemies for a hypothetical and unachievable desire for father, poor thing, so far from knowing and tasting your and my kinks. I miss you. You left sixteen years ago! You forbid me to look for you. I only have your P.O. Box number. Why? You said in your letter, two years back, that after 40 you will live in eternal chastity. You are 40 today. And you feel betrayed and full of anguish. Eternal chastity... I don't know why, but I think you're lying. As for feeling betrayed, we are all betrayed, sooner or later. Full of anguish? Someone very illustrious wrote: "outside the body there is no salvation." Do you know that some youngsters have a special appreciation for wiser and therefore older women? Make yourself beautiful again, my dear, resume your milk and nectarine baths, massage the rose with tiny pomegranate leaves dipped in sweet almond oil, reactivate through this process the natural moistness of your purse, your poor pussy so without pursuers. Together, you and I once again, will be unbeatable. Cheer up. There are exceptional young men exuding exceptional desires.

II

You guessed it. How much we are alike, you and I! You ask who he is. Very well. His name is Alberto. I call him Albert *because of* my dear Camus. The one and only. He is handsome like him. You wouldn't like it if I called him Albertina, right? Incidentally, as you know, Albertina really was the driver of Marcel, the sickly genius who bludgeoned and blinded rats. With very few exceptions, writers in general are disgusting! My taste is for books, but of course I cannot call Alberto "The Plague," or perhaps even "The Happy Death." But let's talk about a disturbing bit of evidence about the masses and so genuinely transparent to me: how the macho men love one another! Why do they make of this fact such immense mystery and suffering? Forgive me, Cordélia, but unless it were you, my sister and so beautiful, I did not have a clear and urgent desire for a woman. But I always like to be sucked off. So sometimes I seduce some of them with little curled up lips. But the phallus in the pink, in women, only *in extremis*. In all women there is a languor, a letting go, that discourages me. I like hard, slender bodies, buttocks like those still green buds, tenaciously attached to their case. I like long feet, stretched out, I hate those women's feet that I saw tending more towards cute or puffy-plump until they're almost square or round. I like a man's ass, manly asses, some black or blondish hair all around, one twitching, one closing itself full of opinion. And women with their moans and their chatter and big red assholes do not turn me on. The buttocks almost always voluminous, half collapsed even if they are young, they always make me think of Pascoalina there at home, do you remember? She would wash mother's linens, her big white butt, wet, pasty, a nauseating balancing act. A woman's ass should serve as good steaks in case of an avalanche. Did you read about such people who ate their favorite frozen guyfriends or girlfriends? Do you remember that other guy, a Japanese man, who literally ate his little Dutch lover? Only there was no avalanche. He even ate her at home, and after having spent some time in the asylum when he got out (not sure why he got out) said: I was misunderstood. And how can you understand someone who literally eats someone, without either avalanche or snow? Returning to buttocks. Yours. Golden and fresh. You were unique. Your buttocks also. Strong, tall, perfect as a boy's. As for Albert. He's 16. He's a mechanic. Do not make that face and do not laugh. If you saw him, your labia minora and majora would swell with pleasure, just like they swelled under my fingers when I played with them, pretending to crush the rosy little pulps. Are you wet? Would you not want Albert's cock going back and forth in your yellow starfruit-loquat-hole? With me you would ask: wait! hold it there! wait a little longer! You would cry. Come.

III

Do you remember how when I was 14 I would go at night to kiss father's feet and sometimes suck his big toe? You would say: "But of course he knows you are sucking his big toe, he must crap himself from laughing." But I'm certain he did not know. I would see him snoring in lovely tranquility. How beautiful father was, no? What thighs! You, at 24, were always masturbating yourself on weekends when he began the endless tennis matches. Dad: what's wrong with you, Cordélia, every weekend you have that face, dark circles under your eyes, a tiredness as if you were playing tennis and not me. And he hugged you. That's when you came. He never understood that dismount of yours at the moment of embrace: you're very sluggish, all crumpled up, daughter, what's happening to you? Poor father, if he knew of your nocturnal raptures, his underwear you stole. Pascoalina: Sir, your underpants are always in the girl's drawers, how can that be? And mother always thinking that poor Pascoalina is the one who mixed up the drawers and rooms: oh, she is somewhat diminished but she washes the delicates so well! Cordélia, do you think we are hateful and cursed for having been what we were? Everyone, incidentally, must think so, because they have not read Rank. You still have the books I gave you? What an admirable human being! What luxury of knowledge and fantasy. I adore him. Had I known at that time that such a man lived, I would have given mine, even if it cost me an enormous hole in the rear. A man of such quality could only have had a gigantic dick, a wise and mighty catfish busting through asses and hearts (how lucky for Anaïs!). There were thinking people on the planet, but everything remains the same. Where are these gods? In the nothingness, in the light? Sister, I feel myself dead almost always. Only horniness, the splendor, the scintillation, the powder is what wrenches me from the sameness. Life here in the city is an endless tedium. The same faces circulating through the night, and when a stud appears from somewhere else the riffraff surge up from all sides, they don't even give a second to get a whiff of him. But Albert is shy, clean in spite of being grease-stained. Imagine: he has eight little brothers and takes care of all of them. What thighs Albert has! Superb! You can see it by the tightness of the pants. And the big balls, and the cock one imagines he has! But I think it is going to be difficult. There are studs full of *entrechats*, turning themselves around, exhibiting themselves, but if you approach directly, they close up shop, safes tightly packed, but always behind panels, in hindsight, I think that anyone but a fool can break into them. I am no fool, am I, Cordélia? Come. Wouldn't you like to leave your cloister there in the countryside and visit me and get to know Albert? I feel your absence. Frau Lotte is still alive and is here with me. Franz, the driver, too. Home and car are very well taken care of. Wouldn't you come?

P. S. Cordélia, and what if I were to write to Albert: Dear one, I don't know whether you understand words and things (that phrase sounds familiar, sister, ah, now I know, the brilliant pervert Foucault). I've been exasperated. Franz has already brought you a pile of notes and you offer no response. How would you feel if I invited you to my house? I know how to make lovely drinks. Do you drink? (Remember this one, irmanita? *The Buck*? We often drank it... 1 1/2 shots of brandy, 1/2 shot lime juice, 3/4 shot of creme de menthe, ginger ale or lemon-lime soda and some seedless grapes. And if the stud only drinks beer? I ask Franz what face he makes when he receives the notes. And the idiot Franz gets stiff and stutters... fface, fface... fface like always, dirty fface... He's a beast, that Franz. He's still a Nazi. He smooths out ancient Second World War magazines, and, by the way, he must have ejaculated onto those pages because they are all wrinkled up, the pages where you can see the Führer with his big arm extended.) Listen, Cordélia, and what if I were to say: I know you have eight brothers and that you are supporting them and I would like to get to know them and help you. Will the stud take all my money? I can skip the bit about the brothers and say only: Albert, I'm just a lonely man, someone who needs a friend. Is that affected, sister? Well, he may answer, sir, I'm just a mechanic, and I don't have anything that might interest you and what's more: I'm a man. Will that be it? Dear, I know you hate these little things of mine, but I am unsure when the prick pleads. And it's pleading: Albert! Albert! If you saw that hard ass, my sister! What perfect buds! The Creator, when he wants to, knows what to do with his hands!

IV

BELOVED: FRAU LOTTE just served me doughnuts, orange juice, waffles, coffee and scrambled eggs here on the winter terrace. While she is serving me small odorless firecrackers go off and she continues serving as if she didn't hear them. She pretends to be deaf and old. I know she gets up to mischief with Franz while I take my brandy after dinner and sometimes, when I'm bored enough I take my naps with the book of a crazy person in hand, one by a certain Daniel Schreber. It's necessary that I speak with you about him soon, or from this point a bit, or perhaps not speak, but the man was very important, a Supreme Court judge or something like that. It is assumed that he began to grow paranoid by the evidence of knowing himself or of feeling himself a passive homosexual. The things of the circle, the little black spot, are very complicated. If they summarily accepted the black hole, if they rolled it up a lot more like many want, the sun would shine again for these poor sick people. Such a one as Schreber talks a lot about the sun (he imagines himself being fertilized in the circle by the rays of the sun! What a dark round luminous son would emerge!), he speaks of the fundamental language, which comes to be a language with its own syntax, which omits words, leaves sentences interrupted and incomplete grammatical expressions, things that I am many times tempted to do and I don't do them but I will end up doing if I continue reading that toga-wearing faggot. It never mattered to me to give up the ass or I think it's of no importance. You also don't, isn't that right, Cordélia? I

Letters from a Seducer

remember very well your yelps of pleasure with my big blunt slipped inside there. But the learned ones say that, for the man, giving up the little black spot is *tutta un'altra cosa*, massages the prostate, they say (it's true, I've even howled several times when the dick was a fist). The explanations are dull, far too technical and I do not want to comment on them at this time. If you have any interest (why would you have?) I can send you a book by João Silvério, *Perverts in Paradise*, a masterly treatise on all that has to do with the orifices and what is attached to them. I return to Frau Lotte. The other night I was heading to the bathroom to do my ablutions (as the bishop would say) when I heard whispers in Lotte's and Franz's wing of the house, and out of sheer childishness decided to inspect. Both of them were drinking nicolatchka. Have you already drunk nicolatchka? Cut yourself a little slice of lemon, put sugar on the slice, put the slice in your mouth, chew it, and soon after drink the cognac in a single gulp. It's an alpine skier's drink. I was close to the wall. I heard:

Franz: he iz horrny for zat nazzty guy.

Lotte: vat nazzty guy?

Franz: ze beauty who fixes ze carr.

Lotte: mein Gott!

Franz: vat a nazzty lott it all iz!

Lotte: Oh poor little Senhorrr Karl und little Cordélia... Senhorrr Karl hat very little time mit die mutter,......ze poorrr little zings, and ze girl Cordélia zo much wizout a head... Und wizout mutter everyzing ends up verrry sad. You had mutter, Senhorrr Franz?

Franz: Zanks to Gott not having mutter, nein senhora, und also not want to speak about mutter mit the senhora, want to speak about ze large acorns of her round breasts.

I tiptoed out and still could hear Franz's guffaws and Frau Lotte's sobs-giggles-farts. Listen, Cordélia, seriously: you told me in your last letter that Albert's balls and cock and little asshole are of no concern to you. That you're not interested any more by all this filthy sex stuff. I feel you're lying. But anyway, you said "filth." And then you talked about "feelings." But please, dear irmanita, you never had them! Are you calling 'feeling' what you were exuding for father? Hanging around the room's terrace, behind that B. Giorgi sculpture, massaging your pussy while papa played doubles, are you calling that a feeling? I had reached my lovely 14 years, you your 24, I was lifting your satin nightgown and standing up screwing you in the ass right there behind the statue (the sculpture there before), while you were masturbating yourself moaning, babbling childish things that always ended in Ohs, Ahs, and you were squatting, crouching down, finishing all sprawled out atop my harmonica, howling, howling, and that never stopped. Later still I licked you, you lying beside the stone vases, and the ferns concealed your view of father on the court, and you propped yourself up on your elbows to see him better, then you saw him... and you would jump up (I still with the tongue hanging out) roaring: bravo papa! bravo! Father saw you break out onto the room's terrace as if you had just gotten out of bed. He said: Oh sleepyhead! have you seen my beautiful playing? Poor thing! And you would throw him kisses and he would restart the match, and you would fall back into bed all sweaty and still moaning, I adore him! I adore him! Come

Letters from a Seducer

on come on, Palomita, are those feelings? It surprises me that at your age you call these riots feelings, this brawling as my friend Piva says, this disorder this mess, this rolling up this shattering of the body, you sentimentalize dicks, you never sentimentalized anything, even these descriptions of yours of birds and plants and sunsets smell to me like a good dick. If your being there were profound, clear, conclusive, you would be happy with your own solitude, proud is how you would feel at being far from the rioters, civilization's garbage, the shithole of progress, you'd still be beautiful because you'd be appeased by the soul's choice and worthiness, and according to what you reveal, you're corroded inside, empty, anxious, and moreover: that you don't read anything any more? that you embroider silver cloths and little tablecloths for charity bazaars in the surrounding villages? Villages? But where are you anyway? By God, irmanita, who are you now? And your thighs, where did they go? Those superb dark devastating thighs! I know women exquisite women in their 40s, taking care of themselves since 30, getting mini-plastic surgeries every year, they have the most gorgeous young lovers or very elegant and amazing 40 somethings! rich ones, my dear, rich. I know, you will say that you do not need money, fine, but what if you did need it? And if the stallions get sick? These beautiful horses of yours can go limp tomorrow, I know it, and what if instead of taking care of horses you took care of a distinguished well-hung man, a healthy pauper, the type that carries crates of vegetables in Ceasa early in the morning? Everything for a prick, Palomita! you'll flourish, bloom, blossom as they say in good writing. And your breasts, Cordélia? You didn't have children, they should be in the same place as always. Let me touch them, suck your nipples, rub the tip of my banana in those dark mammaries. I should stop. I arranged a polo match. The Equestrian Club is a den of delicious and dissolute young studs and lascivious women. Polo and horse... well yes. They go there to bare it all, excite themselves with the smell of men, stallions and mares. And speaking of polo the hundred trees you ordered cut are called willows (I found out) and only a fool plants them near the house and the wood is good only for making polo balls or tiling a roof. Now I ask you: who should want so many polo balls? Who knows, you could export little balls for the entire planet. Anyway. Let there be horses and clubs. I will order a hundred.

V

DO YOU REALLY THINK, CORDÉLIA, that a god was going to look after someone who was eating an apple there in Mesopotamia? What do you feel guilty about? To what sins are you referring? Those innocent diddlings thinking about Dad? Are there other things that I don't know about? And who is this Iohanis that cuts down your willows? Only if the fool sowed them... Are you telling me you've got a man out there who is good, decent, and you are not fucking him? Lady Chatterley's lover was also good, decent, but he put his dick to work, that one called John Thomas. Describe it (the piece) in detail in your next letter, please. You are utter reticence, vagueness, lukewarmness. Don't you trust me anymore? I didn't understand what you meant when you say that you look at the sun. Be careful. That judge, Daniel Schreber, began having conversations with the sun and started freaking out. He said that its rays fertilized him through his little black butthole. I have already told you, Cordélia, to stop this nonsense of looking I don't know how at the sun. Look for Iohanis's balls. They should be around there somewhere, and you aren't noticing them. As for the terrible memories that you have of daddy I find that very strange. Why terrible? Because you feel guilty for having desired him? This all seems to me so outmoded and so annoying. Even I desired him. That golden chest, those golden thighs, those yellow-gold eyes, ah! I know, you continue to adore daddy... the sun. I don't believe, Cordélia, that at 40 you continue on with this travesty of a mania. If you had fornicated with Daddy (I would hate you)

you would be saved (did you screw?) because there is always some defect, a fart by who knows during a fuck, one picking his nose thinking no one is watching and suddenly they catch you reeling out snot. True, unlikely for daddy, but he was human after all... and do not make that face in disgust when I say these things because then I remember Gretchen here at home, a young gal that Frau Lotte hired ("beccause I am tired of looking after everyzink in zis big haus all by myzelf") to help the gal ("who is poor") who vomits when she sees Dog's crap (he's even called Dog and as a matter of fact he's a saint) and at night she licks her boyfriend's hole, a certain Joe the Louse, who brings the groceries from the market. Get this, this guy is called Joe the Louse. And Franz came to tell me that he saw the girl on her knees licking the big black's booty, near the wall, in the midst of parrot beaks, that foliage, you know. Franz: zat girl Gretchen can not shtay here because she likes to lick ze azz of zis Joe ze Louse. At that moment I was distracted and did not quite understand, I thought that Franz was referring to Genet and responded: there were no lice, Franz, they were those pubic lice of Genet, and who is Gretchen? and I was already going to expound on the "Holy Comedian and Martyr Genet" when he enlightened me. I have to stop for today, I arranged a meeting with Albert. Soon I'll tell you more. Brighten you up.

VI

IRMANITA, CHECK THIS OUT: he was tense, tight, unsure. He. Albert. He said yes to a beer with me (I detest beer), he drinks only beer. He is more towards the stocky side, tight T-shirt, a seahorse tattooed on his arm, hairy forearms. He is beautiful in his smile, balls and other endowments (see reference in letter III). Amazed: he has the most perfect teeth. His mother was Portuguese, because no Brazilian without Portuguese or Italian or etc ancestry ever has teeth. You know how much the bastard Heliodoro (!!! My dentist) charged me for a front cap? Forty thousand dollars. Now everything's based on the dollar in our country of pulps pigeons pointers and pleats. You know about all that, or you're turning into Goncharov's Oblomov, a disconnected lump, and are just like him? Yesterday before going to meet Albert, on the way, I came across these scribblings on the wall: death to dentists! And just below it: Oh toad's ass Oh lagoon's ass, I'm good. Brazil!!! Oh naughty land! Today I heard on Radio Eldorado that a Pernambucan who is in Kuwait refused to leave there, with the war and everything, saying he would rather be at the mercy of Iraqis than to come back here. Just imagine his pathetic life here. Well, these topics nauseate me, nothing more to say. Let us return to Albert. We sat at a round table, very cheaply made, I chose a tacky bar (a macho thing in the stud's eyes) and a scrumptious amply-hipped girl passed by, he looked a good while and I as well, I pretended I was interested and started a raunchy conversation, talking only about women. That I love them, that my lust is pathological, that I need to tear open a new one several times a day, that I do have a lover but she's married, that I'm afraid to pick up women out there, all this AIDS-related stuff alarms me and because of that I always have to masturbate. I cited several men illustrious defenders of masturbation, John C. Powys, Havelock Ellis, Theodore Schroeder etc. But I spoke with much brilliance, with much elegance, slightly agitated, occasionally passing my hand on his thigh like a very manly man, sympathetic, relaxed. I described wonderful moments of getting it in and when I detailed an uncommon position (do you want to know, irmanita? She with legs open at the edge of the bed, me licking her and under the bed another woman sucking my pod) he laughed with pleasure, made nervous movements with his leg, and I glanced at him and visualized the dick stuffed inside his pants. I asked abruptly: you never masturbated with your friends?

him: yes when I was a little boy.

I: I'm saying now, as a man.

he: (drily) no.

I continued with similar themes but I largely focused on masturbation, also telling him that fantasy is man's best friend (he laughs) and suddenly on the fifth beer I was incisive:

We gonna pluck the thrush there?

He liked that, laughed a lot at the phrase "plucking the thrush."

He: (smiling broadly and asking for the sixth beer) Why not? Irmanita, I got excited, my wish was to grab his piece right there, open his furrow up and stick my club in that

Letters from a Seducer

assuredly hairy hole. But I was elegant: I got up quickly but with discretion, paid the bill, walked beside him and toward the car, my hand amiably placed on his powerful shoulder and on his little sea horse, opened the door of the Mercedes...

He: It's the first time I've sat in a Mercedes for real.

I: (thinking to myself) also the first time that you'll sit on a table leg. (Or not?)

We got into the car. I do not know how I managed to drive to a dark little street.

I: How about plucking that thrush right here right now?

he: (some tension, smiling) why not?

Then I dared: how about you opening your fly, big boy?

he: (very calm but laughing) why not?

I found that calmness surprising, but it was not me who was going to enter into a dialectic about it. Then I saw: the rosy mallet, lustrous, dewy. My mouth fell on it. He was stripping off everything. I plucked my thrush while sucking that magnificent bat. He sweated and moaned with abandon. Beauty! Rosy! Lustrous dew!

he: (very serious, after drenching my mouth) I never let a guy suck my piece.

I: (dead serious) I understand. I also never sucked anyone's piece.

he: (looking me in the eye) lie.

I: (looking into his eyes and pretending to be irritated) what is it, man, why do you think I'd lie?

he: (almost a little sad) because if it is... then it's strange, no?

I: (neutral) you upset?

he: (nervous) why? I didn't give up the ass, the balls! Look, it's better you leave me at a bus stop up ahead because nobody has ever seen a car like this where I live. It'd attract attention.

I launched into a theatrical tirade, half crazed, but somewhat sentimental, somewhat awkward, somewhat shy (I'm moving when I attempt the genre) more so than rational, and said to him: these things happen, man, so what? I think I got a bit emotional about you. Perhaps I might have fallen for you. I stopped at a red light. Lit a cigarette. And he was (imagine, Cordélia!) crying. Poor thing! How adorable these kids are! What naive little souls! A weepy little thing, Cordélia! What hungry little bodies! What modest neurons! I place, as always quite naturally, my hand on his thigh, and risked a fluid "forgive me," and shortly thereafter a "I think I offended you." He: what? Me: (translating) I think I offended you with my "outbursts." He: what? Me: (translating) offended you because I sucked you off? Cordélia Oh, maybe I should start using that fundamental language of Schreber? Anyway, I left him at the bus stop. Little weepy one. I leave you here too, irmanita. Until soon.

Letters from a Seducer

VII

CHI! MY DEAR, YOU HAVE NO IDEA! That story about Joe the Louse turned into a mess! I hate that rabble. It's necessary to show expressions of comprehension, pity, it's necessary to be very careful, because anything that comes out of your mouth about these people, all these really insincere types will jump all over you. You give them a home, food, clean clothes etc. and they hate you. Then the compassionate ones come in: it is perfectly rational that they hate you, you are rich, my dear, have everything, and these bastards are the forgotten of the world. If I had someone who gave me food home laundry and even paid me, I would suck his cock or her poompoom until the end of time. These kinds of hierarchies have always existed. Differences... balls, nobody has ever solved anything. Napoleon tried. He ended feudalism. He gave little plots of land to many. But what a catastrophe years later! And to think that the monarchy returned after the French Revolution! All that bloodshed for nothing. There you have it. And it isn't up there with the cherubim angels archangels higher authorities? And there in the heavens, seated on the throne of gold, isn't there That One? Hierarchies all the way down to microorganisms. Read the entire Koestler and you will understand everything. Arthur. *The Reasons of Coincidence.* Well, back to Joe the Louse. The guy does not conform to the rumors that spread throughout the neighborhood, of Gretchen being seen licking his ass. The most peculiar thing is that Gretchen, protected by Frau Lotte, doesn't care. She continues to dust everything well and makes little giggly faces the whole time. I, very stern. Frau Lotte came to talk to me. I pretended to know nothing even though I'm aware of all the details, because Franz takes care of that. The true story, according to Franz, is that Gretchen is hopelessly in love with Joe the Louse's tacky ass and with Joe the Louse completely. You needed to see the type. He's skinny, nervous little behind, big nose, smile full of dentures but they are very well done. Someone paid for his dentures. There are people who will pay anything just to lick a little ass. Speaking of which, have I already told you about a friend of Tom's, who is a cousin of Kraus, who sobbed uncontrollably because Kraus would not let her rim him? The woman is addicted to licking cracks. Kraus screeched rudely: here no one touches anything, baby. Later, when that one returned to insist, he responded with guffaws: you little freak, my religion doesn't allow, so don't insist, my guides would not approve. Every time the woman threw herself into Kraus's bailiwick, Kraus laughed so he could have died. He keeled over laughing so hard that he even had convulsions. The other day the woman bristled: either you let me lick the hole or nothing else'll get done, I'm not fucking you any more, I'll split. Can you believe then that Kraus could neither respond nor say goodbye, from laughing so much? He was telling it to us in convulsions: it is not possible that someone has fallen so hopelessly for my backbackbackbone! So now if someone says to him: tell the story of that one who's a friend of Tom's who is your cousin, he starts laughing dangerously. All his friends are now asking for people not to talk about Tom's friend anymore. Kraus might suffer a syncope. The case is serious. He's currently getting therapeutic treatment. I mean, "he tried to do it." He went to three therapists, but those guys also could not stop laughing.

Finally, a problem. And Tom's friend (beautiful, by the way) was "called" Amanda, yes, "called," because now everyone else calls her "The Little Butthole." The story did not stop there, because every time someone sees Amanda, they say: Here comes "The Little Butthole"—and whoever is nearby and doesn't know the history, there's some new person who has to tell it. A mess. Returning to Frau Lotte.

Frau Lotte: Senhorrr pleaze do not belief zat schtory about Senhorrr Joe ze Louze.

Me: (Pretending ignorance) What story?

Frau Lotte: Nein nozink happent nozink mit zat, ze real zink vat happent vas zat Senhorrr Joe ze Louze hat a huge boil in hiz back partz und Senhorrita Gretchen only vanted to repppair Joe ze Louze.

Me: (Pretending alarm) How is that, Frau? Gretchen wanted to *rape* Joe the Louse?

Frau Lotte: Nein it'z nozink like zat... mein Gott, mein Gott.

And then she asks me to get Senhorrr Joe the Louse ppleeaze he will explain everything to me. I found it too much, irmanita. I had one of those fits you're familiar with and said to the Frau that I couldn't care if that Joe the Louse committed suicide with a shot to the temple. Frau Lotte threatened to leave with Gretchen and everything. So I bought her a beautiful piece of English gabardine fabric that she could use to have a suit made by my tailor. Afterwards I pontificated: I never want to hear of these "twatttz" in this house again. One thing, Palomita: please explain to me your "glimpses" of daddy, your nightmares. What are you insinuating? Nothingness making itself into guilt I think. Or not?

VIII

AH, I FEEL LIKE A TEENAGER, Cordélia. He was with an umbrella waiting for me in the rain. He was not singing but was there almost hidden on the small terrace of a really old empty house two blocks from the mechanic's shop, on the terrace where I saw a tire lying against the wall. Albert tells me the tire belongs to "that one there" and points out to me a very impoverished type, a bum. The tire is his nightly pillow. Ah life! Well, I began saying to Albert that that bit of putting it in the fly-hole or giving up the violet patch has nothing to do with conscience. Yes, because he had said before: I have a heavy conscience. Poor little thing. And then I tired of my own eloquence and exploded with a final speech on balls flowers, gardenias and total crap and concluded screaming that I was done with protecting asses and cock, that I didn't have any more time for being the *grand seigneur* and *pas de deux*, spins, beats of butterfly wings, tremblings, that the roar of life had stuck to my chest, thus it was, my boy, in living color, and I showed him my rock-hard dick, angry I seized his balls and... see, Cordélia, he started to cry once again. I was annoyed, because crying to me has something noble about it. I would cry only if God did not want my yessir. Or if he only showed me his tongue without letting me suck it. Petite arrived. Did I tell you about her? We'll talk soon.

P.S. I ate her out in the position I call "The Decapitated." It's like this: the head totally off the bed (remember our beds here at home, towering), the right leg up. You need to be gentle in order not to dislocate the neck of your male or female partner. I was rough. In addition to the moaning it left her with a mildly stiff neck. And did you know Franz knows Genet by heart? How can he confuse head lice with pubic lice? And do you know that he even read *The Death of Ivan Ilich*? The Germans surprise me every day. After "that one" I thought they read nothing more, just prayed. I am outraged. Genet and Tolstoy read by servants. Where are we? What times! I kiss you in the dove.

IX

CORDÉLIA, FOR SOME REASON you insinuate things I know nothing about. You talk about how healthy father was. Nonsense. Healthy is me. And with this hypothetical healthy you insinuate some terrible things I know nothing about or think that they really aren't the same terrible things. Those, I know about. Speak clearly: did you fornicate with father? Was I fooled for all these years? Did you exclude me from the pleasure and hate of hearing your stories or seeing the facts? You're a guilty crybaby why? You remember those clowns I sculpted in clay and then dressed in white satin and colored ribbons? That's how I feel. And what do you mean with this "if I remember Nietzsche at the end," he crying on a crowded street by a broken-down horse? Yes, I remember. And so? I'm no Nietzsche, nor am I the horse, nor am I Lou Salomé. You think I'm crazy? Or that I identify with horses and baronesses like you, Palomita? Pay attention. I can be cruel if screwed over.

P. S. I insist: why do you speak of Nietzsche? Why do you think I'm compassionate gentle cruel and crazy like him? And I ask you: talented too? That I should dedicate myself to letters because you feel I am a writer? Without a doubt you want to offend me, Cordélia.

X

IF IT'S POSSIBLE, if everything that I'm thinking or better everything that I'm concluding is feasible, you and father slept together and rendered me a *clown*. What do you mean by "healthy in bed?" Now I see a certain type eating watermelons, popcorn, splayed out drooling, soiling the sheets, filling them with seeds and peanuts. Certainly this was not father. Cordélia, I'm irritated. You continue to be a fool. When you were young you existed only to get off. You were really stunning. You, yes, something to see with your health, with your watermelons, to be sucked dry. The word "healthy" in relation to father is frankly silly. Father's youthful appearance hid a passionate man, tormented down to his marrow (as the abbot would say). Yes, I received confessions from father... Strange you insinuate the bed, and as I understand it, his *ejaculatio precox*. Do you speak of shyness too? You didn't confuse your partners, did you? Many things were said to me... the youthful appearance, the sportive air, were very well-constructed masks... father was a perfect seducer, a winner, molding himself like water to get what he wanted. Tennis... now, Cordélia, do you really think father was only an accomplished tennis player? A poor little thing in your eyes because he didn't notice you? Foolish thing... Aren't you jealous of someone? And you think mother left with the other one, that doofus, to defy father? Silly girl... Father wanted her to go! And why do you think father was using tennis balls more than his own balls? Of course, the berries should also be used to rub the pussy... well... he did not use the berries with mama. But Cordélia, incredible, you don't remember mama anymore? Those big innocent eyes and her entire body a lovely rotundity, the most perfect nose, arms and hands of Madonna, but not a whit not a whit of a slut. And a woman in bed has to be a bit whorish, remember what Lawrence says: "the woman who doesn't have in herself the least trace of a prostitute is, as a general rule, but a dry stick." More or less that. Mommy rolling those blessed chestnut eyes, immense yes, but perfect for receiving the angel's visit. Her powerful hips always covered by copious linen... her hands at the piano playing *Lieder*... and on the harp, arpeggios. Do you think someone can properly fuck (and by properly in this case I mean nastily) with someone who insists on playing the harp? Because remember she insisted. Did Messalina play the harp? Did Cleopatra play the harp? Did Lucretia play the harp? I doubt it. But I'll check. And now I remembered Mirra who got drunk and seduced Ciniras the king, her father, and had a son by him. Mirra, yes, it's she who perfectly illustrates the so-called Oedipus complex. Poor Oedipus! He didn't know the other was the mother. Neither Freud nor Jung read Ovid (*Metamorphoses*). Anyway. Were you Mirra sometimes? You would not have the courage. Or it's I who know nothing about women. Returning to Mother, she only wanted the harp between her thighs. And father would show up gorgeous, all sweaty from doubles, those magnificent golden thighs, throbbing from exertion, from victory, the lustrous band atop his forehead, beads of sweat dripping brightly, the laughter full of perfume and hunger for another mouth and then... Mom. The dress of white linen and "little beehives" on the collar... Do you also make little beehives on your cloths for those village bazaars? And do you want to know, from me, what sexuality was for father? Here you go: jellyfish hyenas birds juices griffins satyrs bogs ratchetness rattles and mainly

Letters from a Seducer

(calm, irmanita) João Pater, the black man he loved. Did you calm down? Then I'll continue. He found him I don't know where, either in Olinda or Salvador, he was by that time on those tours, and one day, early in the morning, walking around the city he was seized with jubilation with everything he saw, the smell of fruits, the gaping blue of the sky, a jackfruit opening slowly before him... he therefore even said "a jackfruit slowly opening up before me" and suddenly near the fruits, the jackfruit, under the sun, him... João Pater. The black man was distractedly caressing his thighs, sitting down, his legs open, looking at his own hands coming and going on his thighs. Someone offered João Pater an orange. He looked at father and said, do you want some? Yes I want some. João Pater took the knife from his pocket and began slowly peeling the orange. He cut it into two halves. We want some, yes? And he gave half to father. João Pater was 20. Stunning! Stunning! And why did the black man have such a strange name like "João Pater"? Because he took forever to be born, his mother was already on the verge of dying when they summoned the priest named João, and the priest began: "Pater Noster" etc. In the next second he was born. His mother thought the "Pater Noster" miraculous and he became João Pater. The "Noster" she didn't like as much... take your tranquilizers, Cordélia, or a handful of lemon balm, since you already have settled into the countryside and its charms.

P. S. What we are left with is orphanhood. It is not that we miss father and mother. We have been orphans forever. Orphans of That One.

XI

You never saw a black man there at home? Of course, silly, nobody saw the black man. Only him. Constant travel, invented tours. The eternal arpeggios of mother, on returning: did you play well, dear? And you ask how everything was with João Pater, how father said it was? Oh, Cordélia, that it was like a lake acacias, soil, sun, spring, wonder. You're despairing, I feel it. So I should not talk about this anymore. I regret telling you about it. But cheer up: yesterday I dreamed that I was sucking your pussy and you were ascending into the heavens with a harp between your thighs (reminiscent of mom) and the landscape and colors had something of the paintings of Chagall. Then two angels rolled me over like an o and licked me with silver tongues, I could see them (the tongues), I was licked from behind but could see them (the angels) in front as well as if I had a parrot's neck, being able to turn whichever way I went. Then, God himself, with the face of a wanderer or that vagrant with the tire and completely scuzzy, put a tire around my neck that looked like a collar, and was displaying a I know not what (how to name the ostentatiousness of God?), a pink and *kitsch* enough giant chorizo, decorated with tiny stars. I was completely shattered inside. I saw stars (forgive me). I woke up wet and thought: Frau Lotte will see the stain on the sheet. So I got up and went to wash the piece of sheet in hot water. Unbelievable. I cannot even get any peace here at home. I think I'll send the old lady away and hire an innkeeper, an abbess. For don't I have the right or not to soil my sheets without tormenting myself? I felt like I was at

Letters from a Seducer

boarding school. A schoolboy scrubbing up, at dawn, so that the priest doesn't see him. No, Cordélia, do not ask me again, I will not tell any more about father and João Pater. At least if it were orally... Aren't you coming?

XII

IRMANITA: if you were healthy you would come live with me, your brother. You could even crap on my bed and I would not mind. I would wash your little behind and your sheets. But you insist on staying there on your heath. If you were still Virginia there in Cornwall, I would understand. Or one of the Brontës in Haworth, okay. But who are you? No one illustrious. You have no important job to justify your stay in the country. And are you or are you not fucking that Iohanis person? How old is the rascal? Does he cut your trees with the ax or power saw? If it's the ax you are lying when you say you are not fucking that guy. Another thing: I just do not believe your incestuous insinuations. You think a man possessed by João Pater would mess around with you? Okay, there is something hot about being the daughter. But how could he hide those archetypal innocences from me? I felt like father's confidante. And I know he thought you a tiny, sooty little dove, flittering, your eyes like mother's and almost as idiotic as hers (sorry, mommy). Prove it to me. Prove to me that you had in your hairy cavern the big paternal cock and curls, beautiful Mirra. King Ciniras wanted to kill his daughter when he recovered from his drunken stupor. Our father didn't?

XIII

I'M ILL. Taco, my doctor and friend, prescribed chilled champagne. Brut. And ice at the temples. And you know why I'm sick? Because I sense surprises, disturbing news, coming from I don't know where, maybe from you. (And for something else that I'll now tell you.) I also feel that we should not continue with the letters. I see you dissembled, hiding something very serious. Why won't you permit me to come to your house? What are you keeping there? Somehow I have been transformed into a scribe or better, into a scribbler, and just knowing that you think me a writer upsets me to the point of nausea. What petulant types! What disgusting people! They rifle through groins, backside cracks, they rummage in sordid hearts, in shriveled little souls, and then sate themselves with belches when they finish the texts. Truly I love books, but if you could extract from me the vision that these arrogant folks had written I would vomit up the world and life itself less. We used to have a friend, Stamatius (!) (I just called him Tiu, because let's face it, Stamatius won't do) who lost everything, his house and other property, because he had delusions of being a writer. They say that he now lives gathering up as much as he can, he's a garbage collector, you understand? He lives in a squalid cubicle with someone named Eulália who must have been born in the sewer. Many look for him to help him. He doesn't want to know. Tiu wants to write, he thinks only about that, he has freaked out, rushes out in panic when he sees anyone who knew him. He wears on his chest a medal of St. Apolônia, patron saint of teeth. Ah, he no longer has any more teeth. The beautiful Stamatius. Elegant, trim. The last thing he did before disappearing from around here was twist an editor's balls, making him kneel till the guy shouted: I will publish it yes! I am publishing your book! in hardcover and paperback! Only then did he loosen up on the balls and stammer ferociously: go publish yes, but the biography of your mother, that tramp, that piece of ass, that ball-buster, that mangy top-bitch who fucked that donkey father of yours—and broke his teeth with the most accurate blow I've ever seen. He broke his hand. Well, but that doesn't get to the issue. To the worst issue: Kraus died. "The Little Butthole" in a fit of indignation with all the indignities coming from Tom, broke into Kraus's house with her big tongue hanging out, and some say that she pursued him throughout the entire house for a good half hour, wriggling her backside. Reportedly Kraus protected his rim, literally dying of laughter. Do you believe it? He died. Tom wants to prove homicide, he wants the testimony of all the friends and therapists also, but who is going to believe that a guy died from laughing just from the threat of having his button licked? The polo group is considering a plan, some nefarious cruelty toward Amanda. They say that they're going to stuff some polo ball pulps inside her vagina. If that becomes settled send me some of those willow stumps. There'll be balls! Tom was medicated at the hour of Kraus's burial because he could not bear to see his friend dead and still smiling. I'm sick because of all this and because I cannot think about death, not even mine not even Kraus's not even a cockroach's, I'm afraid of that pestilent lady and I imagine myself pulling her clitoris, stretching her pubic hair until I hear tense, horrifying sounds. Today I yelled dementedly: come, Madame, come, and irate, with a jerk, I let go of the pestilent's clit and pubes and they blurred into her lower midsection. If only I could seduce death, lick her armpits, her black hair, drool on her navel, clogging her nostrils with sweetened breath, and say to her: It's me, whore, it's me, moth, I'm Karl, this one who will eternally suck your butterfly if you afford him a long life in the fragrant planet's vulva. Ciao, irmanita.

XIV

SO PASCOALINA would lay you on the living room sofa while Senhora Lamballe and dad were off on tours? And what games would she play with you? Thief? And this happens to be what I imagine: her nibbling your chocha at a leisurely pace... the thief walking right along, walking and suddenly the thief enters the house, i.e., Pascoalina's thumb inside your chocha. Are you telling me that that nauseating Pascoalina masturbated you, you such a little girl? And where was I? Ah, yes, there where I wasn't. But ultimately, from whom did you inherit these crazy acts, these scores, someone touching your cherry and you a tiny little girl all wide open? And what stories are these you mention in which you claim I'm writing things you don't understand and that according to Judge Eliézer the curseword is a solecism of the soul? And who, by God, is Judge Eliézer? If I have a dictionary of obscenities? And I therefore need a dictionary of this kind, I who walked through the brothels of life throughout the entire country? Calling the anus the cibazol, the cipher, the penis the tombstone, the creeper, is a northeastern childhood lifestyle thing, and I don't remember having uttered those terms about any button or any catfish. But in the end is it you who has the dictionary? Or did you mix up your correspondence? You're corresponding with who else? Who knows, are you fooling me and in truth you are a Madame de Staël and you laugh at my letters? I sense cruelty. You're having fun at my expense. You're living there with that Iohanis, your Barbarossa, and I here without drawers, without stud mare, without scarlet eggplant, turning tricks.

Letters from a Seducer

XV

CORDÉLIA, I AM NOT GOING TO NEED the biri stumps. They also call them biris, the willows. They didn't put polo balls in Little Butthole's chocha. Do you know what the punishment was? Licking the a-holes of both teams. Imagine, it was a long match, sweaty asses and horses. There must be sufficient tongue for that kind of thing. Little Butthole was placed in a cubicle guarded and policed by a "good buddy" of Tom's, an enormous type, bulked up, cop's snout, until the match was over. I didn't go in it. After the game I was sipping my whiskey and chatting with some irrelevant types, extremely ancient ladies very much looking to give it up, all covered up, on the hunt. They suffer from idleness. I suggested that they found an organization which I named the SGE, an acronym for what would be the Squadron of Geriatric Extermination. Activity: assassinating corrupt politicians, thieves of the people, and editors of popcorn genre books Jacqueline Susann, Jackie Collins, Danielle Steel. Until they discovered that at the crimes' zero hour there was always an old woman nearby with her poison-tipped umbrella or cane, it would take some time. The police deputy: coincidence, gentlemen, coincidence, the old ladies are different with each crime, or are these men thinking that perhaps there does exist a geriatric extermination squad? Ha ha, and everybody laughs. Everybody competent. Continuing: I didn't go into that Little Butthole's because I found it more reward than punishment. When I expressed my opinion they were furious: it's because you didn't see the state of our cable and curls... What bad taste! And who knows what they really wanted to say with that. I asked that they not say anything more about it because I was eating a delicious plate of toast with salmon. In the late evening after all that they brought Little Butthole out of the cubicle. I went there just to see her face. Can you believe she came out smiling? As if she were drunk. She got plastered from ass! There are inexplicable things with human beings. With the planet too. Outside of ghosts and UFOs. Do you remember the whole Mishima story? I don't want to believe that you have forgotten it. The one who did *seppuku*. You were wrung through with dread when you were reading about it. There were the details: he ate cabbage and thinly sliced raw chicken at dinner the night before. After he stuffed his orifices with cotton rolls so that his feces would not come out at the zero hour. I have a horror of writers. The list of perverts is enormous. Rimbaud, the so-called genius: he would pluck lice off himself and throw them on the public. He urinated in people's glasses in bars. He practically drove Verlaine insane. (And Verlaine's mother? What was the meaning of those fetuses stored in glass jars on the mantelpiece? Writer's mother isn't easy either. Were they Verlaine's little brothers?) Another nutcase. He shot at Rimbaud. If I'm not mistaken, he burnt his own house down. Then Proust: he tells how he stuck needles in the tiny eyes of mice. He beat the poor things. Genet: he would eat the crabs he found in his lover's crotch. Foucault: he'd go out at night, dressed completely in black leather, maybe sado, or maso, giving up and feasting on assholes. Mishima himself, crazy for sweaty soldiers and blood. He got off the first time he saw a picture of St. Sebastian pierced with arrows. Do you know that Franz, not Kafka (Kafka is the most normal one in spite of his cockroach), Franz here at home has gotten quite close to the garbagemen? Every morning I hear a little dialogue:

Good day, Mizter Garbageman, iz ze verk difficult?

Everything straight up, Mr. Franz.

Doing this izn't too nasty for you?

The second garbage man is opening his arms and exposing the bluish tufts of his underarms: what's nasty is dying, Mr. Franz.

Franz leaves laughing, commenting: You really like zese very beautiful garbage men, Frau Lotte, no? and vat amusing hairz und soft tone in ze pitz of zer armz... they look like my people... strrrong, strrrong... Perhaps Franz may be a writer. I'll pay more attention to him. Why would someone like Franz read Tolstoy or Genet? Just one thing, once again: do not insist, Cordélia, that I will not tell anything more about João Pater. And how dare you ask me if I saw the big black man's strap? Father is the one who was seeing him. Not me. What are you insinuating?

XVI

The BONES. The EGGS. The sowing. Those things come to me suddenly with a jolt. I've been spitting in the cracks. I'm filthy, tough even on myself and the world. And confused, Cordélia. A crazy urge to write in the fundamental language. That one. You remember. Of Schreber. Desire to not make sense of some things, some words, of my own life. Thus like life is in reality: absent of meaning. And thus I want to tell you now that I remembered other revolutions. And mothers, women, names, me, us. I remembered the name of the wife of Ramon Mercader. Her name was Orquélia. And you, Cordélia. This has nothing to do with anything. But I remembered. Ramon, from Ra, the sun. And Ramon's mother was named Caridad, a red Stalinist and intellectual author of that monstrosity. Imagine, she was named Caridad! And it was the young son of Caridad who struck that beautiful head. Beautiful, really? New authors refer to him as a raving dictator. Are you confused because I'm recounting all this to you? But it is what Ramon Mercader said when being arrested, or soon after or much later: I was tricked. This "I was tricked" is what resounds, keeps resounding in my ear. Because I was also tricked. That portrait father cut out of the magazine saying it was the Princesse de Lamballe was not true. Did you know? It wasn't the princess. Identical to mom, yes, only I discovered that the person portrayed is named Madame Grand. She was the wife of Talleyrand. In the book of a historian, Simon Schama, there is a picture of that same one, who is not Lamballe, just like the picture here in the living room. I think father wanted me distant toward mommy. He knew that I loved her more than I should. And as the Lamballe history is horrible (in addition to beheading her, they shredded her vulva and made whiskers of it... French people... my God... so refined...), and I, knowing this story, would never lust (in father's opinion) for Mom-Lamballe. He was jealous of me, that crafty bastard! What a family! What lies! And all so *collet-monté* and elegant!

XVII

IRMANITA, KNOWING so little of this Madame Grand (with mom's face) leaves me happy. Maybe I will definitely cure myself of this continuing bad-feeling toward women. So, listen, and see if you come. I'm going to concentrate on snatches very soon. Occasionally I may have relapses because bozó is bozó and eating bozó is just excruciating, excruciating for the other person and good for both. In truth what we want is to tear each other up. They call all this bingeing desire. In nature everything eats. From the lion to the ant. Even the stars devour each other. I shit my pants because of the cosmos. The Creator must have an enormous gut. Some doctors in the sciences discovered that the larger the gut, the more mystical the individual. And who more mystical than God? Large Intestine, pray for us. Speaking of binges I should say that I ate Petite again. She is one of the married ladies there at the Equestrian Club. She's skinny, a redhead, granddaughter of English (why not "Little?") and received from her great-grandfather the first edition of Joyce's book, *Ulysses*. She has been keeping it for years in a lacquer box and hasn't even flipped through it. She is afraid of that monologue of Molly's, says she does not like to get excited by reading of this sort and without anyone nearby. I offered to give her a stroking while she reads. She found it very charming. She's a complete little idiot but has the most beautiful thighs. She smokes those More cigarettes, menthols. Ah, you do not smoke. Nor do you fuck with that one involved with the trees. Iohanis. I don't believe it. Continuing, with Petite. The husband is in Khartoum. Special mission. He is a diplomat or officer of the Foreign Ministry, I don't know. Khartoum. What's in Khartoum? He must collect beetles. He is young, younger than her. All, young or old, the ones there at the Equestrian Club have young husbands. Some pay very well to marry these gigantic studs or slender-elegant types or athletes or stockbrokers. I am a huge slender-elegant athlete and still young, but none of them have caught me. It was difficult to leave the Equestrian Club with Petite without those numerous creepy husbands noticing. They also were following her with their eyes. And without the others, those handjobbers (they all cheat on their husbands and lovers and like jerking men off. Fucking them is more complicated), also noticing. When Petite got in the car I was already passing my hands on her thighs, regal! regal! and unbuttoned her scarlet blouse. There was neither white nor linen nor a beehive. But in hindsight, I would have liked it to have been linen and white like with those little dots, such that Mommy could from now on become an appetizing enough fantasy. Lovely Madame Grand. Well, by the time I stuck my tongue in Petite's mouth, after sucking the nipples of her breasts (semi-droopy, by the way), she told me (Cordélia, see if there isn't really karma, a pursuit): Your tongue is the same as daddy's. How so? I asked. So rosy, so rosy. And how do you know that your father has so rosy a tongue? She was furious: what are you insinuating, Karl? I? nothing, imagine! She told me a long story about the tongue, that her father's was too rosy, everyone noticed when he was slurping up ice cream. Ice cream? But how old is your father? She was furious again. She a complete little lying idiot. She must have sucked that huge paternal tongue like crazy. We know about that, don't we, irmanita? Or did you also only see father's tongue when he was slurping on ice cream? I've been getting a bit angry, yes. I believe and do not believe in your subtle pseudo-confessions. Till when are you going to keep the secret? You say he was not faithful to João Pater. Oh yeah? And the poor black man did not even know. And with things so important to for us to talk about, you ask me for news about Little Butthole. Why? Interested? Well: Little Butthole went to the hospital. Tom discovered that she has a shallow box that only fits a strawberry. He hired two with gigantic dicks to teach her pussy a lesson. Tom can only be in love.

P. S. Was it with you that father cheated on João Pater?

XVIII

PALOMITA, do you remember how you would dip my stick in your cup of chocolate and soon afterward lick the bird? Ahh! your beautiful tongue! I recall every sound, all the landscapes tones those afternoons... cicadas, the black anus (cuculiform fowl from the cuculid family... my God!) and the smells... jasmine-mango, lemon trees... and your movements smooth, prolonged, my movements frantic... Ahhh! Marcel, if you remember, perceived a whole universe with his *madeleines*... He must have sucked that magnificent member of his driver, with *madeleines* and grandparents and teas and all... Ah, irmanita, the mauve curtains, the silver jar, the golden chrysanthemums, some petals on the mahogany table, you dissolved in my half-closed eyes, your breath of chocolate and of... "fertilizing solution" as your judge would say. I've been feeling like a dick of a writer, and when this begins it never ends. What makes me think I probably might be one is that whole perverted story involving father's big toe. A creep of a writer. The other day I told Tom the story of father's big toe, as if it were another guy's story, not mine. You know what he said in response? "If any son of mine had a fetish for sucking my big toe I'd sleep armed." *Ciao*. Petite showed up. She has fallen in love. A nuisance. I will continue shortly.

Continuing. She is gone. Sometimes she is unbearable. She says she loves me but cannot stand when during my "outbursts" I say the word "cunt." I ask her if it is a problem of the moral order or semantics. Her eyes widen, and it is clear that she hasn't the least idea what semantics are, and answers: it's just *disgusting*, baby, nothing to do with morality, there are other words that also sound unpleasant to me.

which ones?

ah, you are going to laugh at me... but I cannot stand the word effusion nor the word abundance... I even grow cold... see, could it be the *u*'s?

but what happens if someone keeps repeating cunt abundance effusion?

oh, baby, please, I might faint, I am not feeling well... don't repeat them...

Really? strange... have you ever fainted?

I almost died when they said all three at the same time... it's something in the ear... it hurts...

I grew radiant. I wished for her death. In bursts surprising phrases came to me. And I began:

There was an abundant effusion of cunts

and in that effusion... the cunt in bed... the abundance on the table...

clear cunts, with abundant hair, sincere effusions

cunts on the table, abundance of nymphets, effusion of dicks

I score your cunt in effusion

sincere effusion, cactus in action, and two goals: rim and cunt

She slipped under the bed, sobbing, I got behind her, nude, I dug my nails in her ass and kept repeating abundance effusion

Letters from a Seducer

cunt, I slapped her several times, until she fainted. When she woke up, I said: I'm repeating: abundance effusion cunt. She smiled. She was cured. Her husband is now in Java (!). To me he is nothing more than an opium smuggler. What are people going to do in Sri Lanka or in Java or Khartoum? Perhaps followers of a new religion. When I ask Petite these things she says: Marcius (!) is curious, he loves to travel... I say: he must like olive-colored clubs. And always beetles—cooches—, of course. The other day I read that a friend of Richard Francis Burton did very badly with a beetle that got inside his eardrum. Maybe Marcius (!) wants just that, to eventually go deaf, because Petite is a radio in bed. Opening her legs already initiates a sickening rant. I try to restrain her by covering her mouth, but she does not understand, thinks it's a fetish of mine, that I like to cover her mouth as if I liked to feel like a rapist, she's a dimwit, poor thing, but she amuses me. Ah! if it were you, Cordélia! We could put a picture of Daddy in front of us (I have some beautiful ones! I can enlarge them...), and we could suck each other, on each side of us a photograph of Daddy. Then I would pour champagne in your pussy, which must be so very dry, poor thing... or not? Or that Iohanis... no, I don't even want to think... and I would suck your little toes, one by one, the little caverns of your ears (do you still use Calèche?) and the little hole in the front and the big hole in the back... come on, sister, I think that you refuse illusions and illusions are life's linchpins. Cordélia, meditate on this: you are going to rot away one day, the worms will gnaw at you, okay, you will be cremated, but that also is annoying, the corpses suddenly seated, you know? because of the heat... that's an oven for you... consider that you are still alive, and I promise to make you very happy like you always were when you were with me, I promise always to dress like daddy, with those Prince rackets and the lustrous headband, and you like Madame Grand if you want, or, just as Cordélia, who is how I would now like you...

Come.

XIX

YOU HAVE GOTTEN UPSET. You ask that I give up. You will never come. And finally you confess: that Iohanis is blond, has golden thighs, is 15 years old, loves tennis and is the spit-and-image of father. I am brother and uncle. You are mother, sister and mistress. Congratulations. So many lies. Slut.

XX

THE LILACS, THE LEAD, the waters' frog-green, your blouses, beloved, smelling of apples, your black underarms, fleshy as small black frogs, I'm confused like Talleyrand before a basket full of heads. So then, Cordélia-Mirra, Iohanis is your son and our brother. You got father drunk one rainy night, alongside the stalls. And thus I saw you the next morning, pale, packing suitcases and bags... I never understood why you left. Now I do. Twenty-four and in love. And pregnant by father. Is brother fifteen, then? And you say I can never see him. You want him only for yourself, Palomita. Very well. It's like a judge (not Eliézer, another) used to say, when he was reproached for screwing his daughters: I made them, I eat them. Can I not have a caracole of Iohanis's hair? Not a couple of his pubes? No kiss? And he is so strong that he cuts down your trees? I cannot even see him sweaty, flushed, or touch his balls? Every day you look at your forty years in the mirror... and you are even more beautiful. You torture me. That he loves you and knows only your pussy... In truth you're feeding on a young sap every day... And for me what remained was going back to Albert, the mechanic guy. He let loose. We tried all the positions last night, after receiving your letter: wheel, jack, pliers, little donkey. I am not going to tell how they are, try them yourself. We also did the "float": I laid out, he on top of the windshield, his arms open and singing "Do not say goodbye to me." He doesn't even cry anymore.

Karl

I, Stamatius, say: I'm getting fed up, Eulália, I'm removing myself from that disgusting Karl.

Eulália: who is this guy, huh baby? he your relative? write the good stuff, gross stuff, nice stuff, or if you don't wanna write what I already told about my life, there's a lot of things for me to tell you, there's things all over the world, go write it, Tiu, write about people I knew there in Rio Fino.

I'm hearing without listening, I ask distractedly: where did you learn to fuck with the grace of a gazelle?

She offers a big smile, completely opens up, she puts her hand tenderly on my shaft and says in low voice: come, Tiu, come on. She has the skill of Madame Grand when she opens up, she's all heat, she's lightness, she's surf, she's beautiful, Eulália when she fucks. I hit the mat, close as possible to her, and adjusting her position she embraces me and says that she knows a dark story, a guy who turned into a dog, and before turning into a dog he was a gorgeous blond "comical even" but was living eating the snatches of the bitches in the street and one day his teeth grew, they were pointy, and he also found himself covered in hair... Won't work for you, Tiu? for the man who makes books?

it depends. he didn't turn into a werewolf?

no. was just dog, ended up over there in the Little Fairy widow's house.

how did he end up there? and who was the Little Fairy widow?

uh, he ended up there, as a dog he was ordinary, a big dog like the others, chewed on bones, that stuff, barked.

I got you. And the Little Fairy?

the Little Fairy widow liked women.

interesting. where was this?

in Rio Fino. and the Little Fairy widow dressed completely in tulle, stood on the doorstep and when the little girls passed by, she would say: pretty little thing, come eat a tapioca cookie.

I got you. and the big dog was there by her side...

that's it.

okay. I am going to write "Tulle, the little lesbian fairy."

no. write about the boy who turned into a dog.

but he only turned into a dog, that's all?

uh. and that ain't enough?

it is. it's something for an editor, but it has to be a raunchy dog, a fucker.

ah, that he wasn't, he was a simple dog, a quiet one.

then it's no good, it must be just SO (and I lick my lips slowly and roll my tongue), a big raunchy dog.

Eulália laughs deliciously. She looks at me as if I existed, nothing looks at me as if I existed, that made me want to eat a sole sandwich now and Eulália for dessert. But I have to write at least one more crappy little story and sell it to who knows what crappy supplement.

know what, Tiu? write a horror story, everyone likes being afraid, people feel something in their gut... a big chill.

okay. so I begin:

HORRIBLE

He lay down. Hoping that all of that would pass. He was afraid of life, of events, of extreme poverty. Sometimes he looked at women. He could see legs mouths teats and knew he would never have them. He watched some small birds in the neighbors' backyard. Guavas. The closest neighbor, Dona Justina, had a sad husband. In the afternoons he sat on the small balcony, looked around and cried.

what's wrong, old man?

it's nothing. it's old age.

I looked at myself. Twenty-eight years. Alone. I went to the window. The old man asked: and the books? Did you uncover something? The old man always saw me bent over books. The table was facing the window, the window opened onto the veranda where in the afternoon sometimes the old man would cry.

you don't want to read a bit to me?

I started reading Camus' *A Happy Death* to the old man. It is the story of a man, Zagreus, who kills a guy to steal all his money, and who goes on to live his life in a beautiful place by the sea. There is no repentance, no remorse, just an eye's worth of tears once, on the train. Or is he the one who remembered Zagreus's tear-filled eye? Mr. Donizeti, my old neighbor, marveled:

tremendous, it is easy to do, fantastic.

you mean that it is easy to kill?

ah, if I remembered someone rich... I had a very rich friend, he was very stingy, deserved to be killed, but he must be dead by now.

but you would be able to do it?

He smiled. He talked about life's immutable landscape, routine, day after day the same steps to the toilet, the room, the bedroom, the balcony. One evening the old man disappeared. D. Justina was shocked:

where did that man disappear to?

maybe he went to the store to buy cigarettes. get a drink perhaps?

what cigarette, what drink, he only drinks coffee, he doesn't smoke.

then a cup of coffee, who knows...

he doesn't leave here for any reason. you didn't notice that only I go out?

At night the old man still had not shown up. I took a few strolls around there, I was asking around, no, no one had seen the old man, nor indeed remembered him.

he never goes out, that it young man?

OK, but you have heard of him.

that he is an old man, yes, who is D. Justina's husband, and sometimes he cries on the veranda, yes, and he's always sitting down

is he tall? someone asked.

Letters from a Seducer

more or less.

is he blond or brunet?

he's old.

does he have any traits? asked a soldier who was passing nearby.

he's sad, I said.

We laughed. The soldier and me. Then, don't know why, I decided to tell that I had read him a story... and that...

a story?

yes... I got worried... a story by Camus, a story in which...

by who?

that doesn't matter, but it's that that story...

The soldier frowned, mumbled something, then said he was in a hurry and needed to report to barracks, etc... But I clearly heard the words "imbecile" and "story." The days passed and nothing of Senhor Donizeti. D. Justina would not leave me alone, and also didn't want to look for him:

know why, Senhor Pedro? (it's my name), I had a nephew who disappeared just like Donizeti, then his mother went to the station, and right after that the boy appeared already dead. Whoever files a report finds who he's looking for, but will find them dead.

you mean that the police will find and kill the disappeared person?

precisely. in order not to give them more work later on.

well, D. Justina, I'll report it, whether you want it or not.

Apprehensive I started straightening up my little room, made the bed, put the books in order and while locking the gate I saw Senhor Donizeti climbing the small slope that was our street. He was approaching laughing, tattered, drunk:

Ha ha ha!, how many I killed, Senhor Pedro, how many rich people I now don't remember and I remembered and killed... ha ha ha... how good it is to take other people's money and go live by the sea... I'm at sea... (uah uah... and he vomited).

but really killed, Senhor Donizeti?

I killed here in the head Oh, only here in the head, so drunk, it's easy to kill everyone, ahhhh, how good it is to drink... how much time lost without drinking! From here on out I am only going to do that, drink drink!

D. Justina showed up screaming. They embraced. I walked, thought: yes drinking. And I kept walking, then took a bus, got off and kept walking... do I get a drink or not? And right in front of me a bar. And drunks. And a woman. All merry, laughing. I sat down at the counter and started drinking. And the fear of life, of events, of extreme poverty, all that passed. Drunk, looked at the woman. I saw legs teats mouth. She: you want to sleep with me? I said yes. Is there somewhere we can go? I said yes. She has been with me ten days. She makes coffee, leaves lunch ready for me and heads out to work in a toy factory. So you really work? I said. And what were you doing that day at the bar? I was sad that day and also decided to get a drink. She is delicately gentle, is 22 years old does not have anyone living here in the city... I have no

Letters from a Seducer

one, I only have a sister but she lives far away, in Trambique Grosso. Where is that? Oh, it's not on the map... it is far away. Now, for the first time she called me my love, and said that as soon as she saw me she felt something here inside, oh, here in the heart. Suddenly, I felt disgusted with that wellbeing, that tenderness, by that woman's potential devotion. Inexplicably I wished she were not there. That she were gone. But how to avoid tears, bewilderment, explain to her that I felt nausea and despair now by her invasion? And as if guided by someone, possessed, I went into the kitchen, grabbed a knife and with one blow killed her. Then I called the old man. Pity, he stammered, she has no money, does she? No. I wrapped her in a sheet and Senhor Donizeti helped me to bury her in the backyard. D. Justina thought that we were preparing a flower bed: coriander, she screamed from the front, cilantro and arugula... a flower bed! That is good. Afterwards, I and the old man drank a bottle of aguardente, and went to sleep. Anesthetized. Something I did not understand had emerged from me. The sun was already high when we woke up. Me and the old man. There was between us only an uncomfortable impression of having buried someone. D. Justina vainly looked for the flower bed. The birds were singing in the guava trees. Something has changed, the old man told me, and that's somehow nice, no? Nice yes, I replied.

Eulália: ay ay ay, Tiu, what a horrible thing, why'd the dude do it? It wasn't that kind of horror I was telling you about! Don't ask me for anything else, write whatever tomfoolery.

TOMFOOLERY

I GOT TIRED OF READINGS, concepts and data. Of being austere and sad as a result. I got tired of seeing frivolities taken seriously and unimaginable cruelties treated with irrelevance, with admiration or utter contempt. I'm old and rich. My name is Leocádia. I decided to drink and screw around before disappearing into the earth, or fire or filth or nothingness. I hired a secretary-companion and said to her: you are young and appealing. When men want to have sex with you tell them to make an effort and sleep with me. I will pay each one of them very well and you will receive princely commissions with each success. She was perplexed. She looked at my still slender but diminished enough figure, asked me to lift my skirt, I lifted it, she looked stunned at my withered thighs. Ma'am, she retorted, it will be very difficult to convince them, but comply I shall, forgive my way of putting that... And she ran out of the room toward the bathroom. On returning she told me she had been a teacher and always felt slight nausea when juggling syntax, but before a subject so repugnant (in her view) plus complex syntax, she actually had to vomit. She was red-faced and tearful but proud. She continued: I will behave in an undignified manner to satisfy you so long as my salary is compatible with such awfulness. I told her the amount. She beamed. Her name is Joyce (!). She is *mignon* and delicious, with a teenager's small breasts, she's 30 but looks 20 (I'm not afraid of syntax), her mouth with slightly raised corners, the light eyes between yellow and brown, hair almost auburn, elegant in gait and posture. Out of nowhere she asked me, in the evening, before my first whiskey (I learned that every drink is less fatal if you start drinking from six o'clock on) if I was familiar with Chesterton. I did not believe what I heard. Was Chesterton some buddy of hers? A teacher? Some politician? No, ma'am, I mean Gilbert Keith Chesterton, English novelist essayist critic and humorist. My God! I exclaimed, I who stopped thinking to continue living, see myself before someone who has read Chesterton. Please Joyce, I warn her, and warn her with a quoted phrase: "If thy head offend thee, cut it off." That's what happened with mine, because for me after all my reflections on the sordidness, the ignominy, the villainy of mankind, I would prefer to forget that a Chesterton existed.

very well, madam, we will not talk about him. Would you like to sleep with a man every day?

no way. once per week is fine. on other days I prefer to have a drink by myself, fart, beat my box, and think about trifles.

what?

forget it.

On my fifth whiskey she had understood almost everything. I explained to her that above all the man should be young. That she would make sure of their potency. That she not send me anyone with a nib or a nub. That with me the man remain mute. That I had already arranged a beautiful pillowcase with French lace to slip over my head. She was astonished. I clarified: my wrinkles are sharp enough, I do not want to scare them.

I think, Senhora Leocádia, that you are being too cruel, just too cruel to yourself.

that's none of your business. I know everything about cruelty. I know God.

I showed her a pair of beautiful blue satin pajamas and asked if she liked them. They're beautiful, Senhora, you want to use them next week? They are for you, Joyce, when the young man is at that point send him to me.

perfect, ma'am.

the roll of money will be there.

where?

in my room. order him to look all around him. he will discover it, money sparkles.

Well, now I want to tell you about my son. He is 40 years old. Married. His wife is a bit of an idiot, one of those who talk endlessly and always absurdities. She read someone who was talking about the importance of "speeding up the spoken concept," of gushing. Her visit was hell. I put on my chestnut-colored shawl and sang in a low voice only for her a funny song from my college days: how is it goat beard / it's been a while since we put it in / it's been a while since we fucked... She completely stood on end. She said to my son: Leocádio, your mother is crazy. how can you leave her here alone when she should be in one of those beautiful places where little old ladies embroider, sing lullabies, fry up dumplings... you've seen the tools she has under the bed?

what tools?

rakes, shovels, hoes... and imagine! a tangle of rosaries!

Letters from a Seducer

Then I explained with perfect harmony between words that the most sensible thing was keeping tools there because the shed in the back could be targeted by thieves and here in my room only the gardener and Monsignor Ladeira come in.

they come in your room? For what?

the gardener to get the tools and the monsignor to pray.

and he does not have his own rosary?

he does. but he can forget it. and here I have others for us to pray together.

Of course all this was not true. Monsignor Ladeira was a great lover but always forgot his rosary and every week would buy a new one. They sent him to Rome. Pity. The tools were a taurus's fetish. He loved the land so much that he could only achieve pleasure if he had shovels rakes hoes there at the foot of the bed. Disgusted with life he went to be a gardener in a convent. A Wittgenstein type. He had a good schlong. But my son seemed satisfied with those explanations upstairs and told my daughter-in-law the cretin: Leocádia is completely lucid. After having convinced him of my lucidity I hostilely hopped around my daughter-in-law and launching spit in her face I repeated my little song without my son hearing me. Thank God, now they don't bother me any more. Leocádio phones me sometimes. Oh, how delicious and practical it is that people think us strange... The comfort of no longer being taken seriously, this farting all of a sudden and smiling as if it wasn't you, and being able to caress a dead fish in the fish market and to cry before a scabied and starving dog. It's good to be weird and old. Well. Joyce has been very shrewd. She meets young men and explains everything to them. The first was a very skinny man, sunken chest but a splendid cock, he looked at the money, stroked it, kept it and smiling told me: I'm always at your command, you see, lady? As he was leaving the room I lifted the pillowcase a little and saw his singed pubic hairs and I asked why.

It's because I was making a batch of eggs and oven-baked potatoes there in the boarding house and the oven exploded.

Ah...

Does this mean that you talk, lady? And see without seeing?

of course, can't you see?

do you have something else on your face to hide?

just old age.

my grandmother is old and I like her.

but you don't fuck her, do you?

ah, but she doesn't have that much money!

I understand.

He left the room. Suddenly he shouted from the other side of the door: I have a friend who is named Tomfoolery who also has an exceptional piece, can I refer him to Joyce? Yes you can, I said. and why is he called Tomfoolery?

a guy wanted give up his ass and a lot of cash to him, and he responded: young ass I eye only and don't put it in. everyone thought it foolish, because with cash people will put it in whatever hole.

Letters from a Seducer

of course. yes you can send Tomfoolery.

what do you know, lady. you are a very sensual old lady!

Tomfoolery also is very "sensual," I thought two weeks later, when I got to know him. I'm happy. I even take off the pillowcase.

Eulália: poor old lady... but she had fun right? now come closer... stop writing, rest, come on... today is Saturday.

SATURDAY

THE DULL. THE DIFFUSE. The tangled. He stole my wife. I will steal his life. He wrung himself opaque, after which he profiled himself in artifices, poses. It's true, he puffed up his chest before females, the nostrils an almost nothing distended because that is how they like them, the neck throbbing immensely. There was finery: designer labels, soft honey-colored jackets, milky speech, the car, the shirts striped blue, the tobacco-colored valise and on Saturdays the racquet, the morning of primroses, contrasts. I have everything. And he was looking at his own musculature, his stone-hard face, blondish hair on his chest his thighs his arms, yes, a joy to feel that way, everything breathing, a suitable life that morning, that one from above, of primroses, of contrasts. He took a gigantic breath, he thought about himself, his tongue full of *recuerdos*, the taste of the beautiful wife, orgasm, the viscous. After the wine, she putting on her stockings, the wife's feet, her nails a slightly silvery sheen and... but why, my God, did I remember an ragged old woman now, smoothing the fish's rough scales, also of a slightly silvery sheen?

you going to take the fish, lady?

And I there on my Saturdays, just passing through, the finest of the fishmongers, tiles, scales, a blue and yellow rectangle recreating the body of a fish, its fleshy scales.

I'm just thinking, boy, how pretty he must have been out there in the sea.

if you're not going to buy move on, lady.

I paused a moment, in all white linen, bermuda shorts, jacket, racquet, and I heard the old woman's tremulous speech.

life is harsh, isn't it young man?

I keep going. The club further up ahead. I enter. Go straight to the courts. And close to the fences, that one my wife, and a friend smiling, touching her mouth, nose, forehead. Did they see me? No. In seconds I rewind the film, I see her, fingers spread between the hair, words loose, indolent...

she: ... so delicate... your friend... seems so wise... young no? you always play on Saturdays?

An explosion of invisibilities, a sound of glass and cracking, and afterwards a languor flowing, one that life's for, yes, I am captured by that woman like my body is captured by its own measure, caught as the comics say, and suddenly I know that abandoned fish, that mortal body. It is harsh, yes, life, Senhora. To think that that exists, death, also for me, imagine, he-I within that space full of freshness, luxurious. Some men were already at the bar and laughs were coming from there, and the scent of expensive colognes, and bells in the women's speech.

I saw your partner... your girlfriend also... aren't you going to play?

Was it true this murkiness, this mire, this diffuseness, this mustiness that was covering the day? He thought about which way he was going to do it, he remembered the book, *Suicide - User's Manual*, no but he wasn't going to kill himself, he was going to kill the other one, the sensitive one and in her words "so wise." Why wise? Zen-adorable airs, mild-mannered, very naive in business, in day-to-day patterns, lazy even, wasn't he looking at the near sunset the day before yesterday through the window panes of the study as if he were dreaming? thinking about what, man? Things are still going round and round out there.

He saw him. He was beautiful, thin, the dark smooth hair, the eyebrows too perfect like those of certain women, a black arch-wing, he liked his friend a great deal, he could say that... and in a second the impulse struck him to embrace him, to breathe close to that mouth, to enter that body, to love him. And he breathed close to that mouth:

it's late, you're right, let's go for drinks like always.

The other one grew pale, tautened the muscles of his face and whispered between his teeth—not today—I reconsider: perhaps he loved the wife because the wife loved the friend. Or was it the contrary? How many times did he speak about him because the wife wanted to? Innumerable ones. Almost always. Was it that that united them? The tenuous, the mild, the almost wise. Thus I want to scream in this morning of primroses and I remember someone in some book "the giants should be killed because they are gigantic." And gigantic was the tumult that he felt, an unnamed portentousness, an avalanche covering stones and bodies, transforming the instant into a warped darkness, a patch of oil on his own face, trickling down. Did he not love his wife?

sweating without playing? we've been waiting for you for a half hour.

Together. Perfect. The golden apple, as in fairy tales. And sporty, slender, clean. And looking at them, a golden

Letters from a Seducer

circle surrounded them, a vast luminousness, frictionless, an enameled body, a smooth muffling. He remembered all the rules of a condensed game, he showed himself polished, perhaps a bit unwell.

if instead of playing we went to the mountain, to my house, there at the summit?

And the knots were tightened, the murk duller, the diffuseness more lachrymose, the entanglement more octopus. And the sweat that trickled was the best pretext for changing from the morning's scenery, so blue, now almost cold.

no game, then? what a shame.

there will be many Saturdays.

He knew that from that point going forward the three would play with a scalding voluptuousness.

Eulália: I didn't understand anything. you ain't gonna stop, Tiu? I'm sad.

SAD

BENT. He used to say strange things when he ran into someone on the street. For example he said: not everything can be fixed. The others looked at him and sometimes responded: true. not everything. Or they did not say anything and kept walking and looking back, fearful or simply surprised. They did not know his name. They said that at a certain point he appeared in town. He was well dressed. A sheaf of papers in his hand. Many papers. In addition to the "not everything can be fixed," he spoke mainly about the difficulty of being understood. The others: you don't speak of anything else besides that... do you live far away? are you lost? did you have an accident? He repeated: not everything can be fixed. And what was on those papers? They looked. Nothing, nothing, just blank sheets. The people of the village became accustomed to him. An old widow boarded him in her back room. The man slept between broken chairs, tarnished mirrors, peeling chests. They asked the widow: did he say something else today? only that same thing: "not everything can be fixed."

One rainy day, in the late afternoon, the man shouted, "not everything can be fixed, fix up what you can." The widow stood on the porch of the house and started yelling enthusiastically: he said something else today! he said "Fix up what you can!" And they were all celebrating at the corner bar. Things were going well when on April 21st, shortly thereafter, the man hollered: I want to fuck! I want to fuck! They tied him to a pole and engulfed him with blows. A dog passed by and watched the man die. Then a young man came and said smiling: that's it, big boy, no fucking no can do. Those who heard, roared. Someone remembered that the man could not stay there dead, tied to the post. An old man called the sheriff. The sheriff called the Mayor. The mayor called the priest. The priest called the gravediggers. They came for him at night. It was raining now. Before burying him, the gravediggers searched his pockets. In the right pocket of his pants there was a faded photograph of a boy holding a pig. Behind the picture was written: my first love. They then buried him with photograph and all.

don't cry like that, Eulalia. I will stop here. in a tricky hollow.

OF OTHER HOLLOWS

> ...an infinitely ruined splendor
> ....the splendor of rags
> and the somber challenge of indifference
>
> GEORGE BATAILLE

To exist is a habit I do not lose hope of acquiring.

EMIL MICHAEL CIORAN

HERE WE ARE. I and Eulália at the beach. We rid ourselves of the garbage, the junk. I sold my books. I'm naked and I look at my beans. Eulália looks at herself. No one around here. Very soon we will sell clams, oysters, coconuts. I return to my hollow. But this time looking for nothing. Only keeping an eye out. I watch for things and chat with my balls and cock. I have only this body. I eye my hands too. Knotty. The right hand still bears traces of the well-aimed blow to the publisher's jackass jaw. My dick still bears its lofty luster. How many times did I put it in you... What burning caves. You slid your head in narrow furnaces, such... that you scraped your temples. Temples and head. I speak to you as if you were people with me. You're blind, broke, and commanded by my great egg of chaotic connections: my head. So like yours now. Lustrous, smooth. Less lofty. I wonder, without waiting for a response, to what do I owe sticking my dick in so many puddles? I remember you, tiny oar, little nib, entering a urinal... What space, you thought, what breadth, what beautiful splashes in all this so wide for me so tiny. And then, I Stamatius swelling, stuck you in vulvas, anuses, even in delicious fags, elegant, blonds, curly haired, others stocky, tall and how many times I took you with my hands, stingy with you, how many times I scrubbed you with soap, pale adolescent Stamatius on the blue tiles dreaming of young girls, rich ones on the corner, with parasols and beach balls, golden pubes, slits showing.

you don't want nothing, honey?

She has a beautiful belly, Eulália. Like a child. Swollen. Has lively thighs. They quiver a little, almost not at all, but they communicate, Eulália's thighs. I ask her to lie down beside me.

Sweetly say to her: open your legs. My knotty hand contrasts with her milky flesh, its girlish and sensitive splendor, such courtesy, Eulália at the start of fucking, such gentleness. She keeps opening up and smiles. The hairs are almost red. What did you do to them?

for you, to stay really light, it's prettier to have blond pubes, huh, Tiu?

I don't say anything but I think yes, Eulália's red pubic hairs have everything to do with my crimson inside there.

After very lazily brushing my finger against her wet pussy: my beautiful cutty, my concubine.

We both smiled and I mount her on the empty beach, in my emptinesses, my fears.

fear of what, Tiu?

of everything... look around... the crab (I imitate it), ugh. I will not talk about my fears with Eulália. So I suck her breasts, the furrows of her ears, narrow nostrils, I pass my tongue over her eyes, lick her whole face, I slobber into her mouth and I'm putting it in, dying, drenched in light and sweat, I tell her all the names, some fleshy reds, some leaden, and she moans and cries almost inaudibly, now a bird, now a bitch, still a little bird, at this exact moment a panther cub, and I look at the thread of the horizon, squinting, steamed up I keep looking, a ship there approaching, closer by the crab again and me looking and coming. Look at him there again. Coming out of the hole. My life has been a coming out of every hole. Leave... imagine, each time I'm in deeper, or leave one and enter another, tiny holes, bigger ones, gigantic ones, and other huge holes full of crap, and me just trying to invent words, me just trying to say the impossible. Eulália gets up and goes looking for clams and oysters. We live at the end of the beach. The house is made of straw and clay. Behind the house the river. Every night we hear the waters' voices. I prefer this, not being anyone, to living with those creeps. How sickening all of them! If you do not lick the ass of those scumbags you are fried. And what friends! That idiot Karl only thought about getting it in. It's common knowledge that, as a little boy, he stuck his nib in his mother's mouth. The mother couldn't stand young Karl. It was stick your finger in your bottom all day. And like it. And suspend himself between the legs of his sister, cling to them like a slimy beast. Enter the mother's midsection. He wanted to be a writer, that guy! That jerk! Day after day picking up and flirting with hot guys in the streets... and women loved him. Fools. Why think of him now? Because the deception and cynicism that exist among people is not easy to forget. And he's one of the first who comes to mind, when thinking about emptiness and depravity. I will devote myself to silence. I will forget I'm human. Can I? All of them swallow each other. Can I stop swallowing? I will keep asking but do not expect answers, I want to continue asking while knowing that I will not hear voices, not even That One's up there above, that traveled a long time ago toward Nothingness. How would this be like permitting no more memories, nor embraces, nor intercourse, how would this be like dying before being dead? Here comes The Trickster, The Whore, The Rascal, Death, wanting me to sample her codfish. Come on, madame, come on, I'm all ready. Suddenly there are lights in my left eye. An orgy of lights. I remember reading that Hildegarde von Bingen, erudite

Letters from a Seducer

woman of the ninth century, saw shards of light and angels and cherubs in the insides of a carnival of colors. Phosphenes, said the sages. And period. So phosphenes in my left eye. I should be lathering up, hurling myself into the river, not to die as clean as possible, but to await Eulália and her basket of clams and oysters. And I should have looked for coconuts and hearts of palm. But I'm here writing with this lone stump and when I stop I'll swap a coconut for another pencil stub over there at Ox Shop (so named because an ox passed through there once and let out a huge fart). They sell cachaça peanut fudge maria-mole dried meat tin cans of sauce. But I should have gone to gather up coconuts, hearts of palm, and I didn't. I keep talking about what I don't want. My fingernails. Tiny and filthy. And my toenails? good to say, they are clean. Eulália cut my toenails with a small pocketknife, imagine. As I am almost not walking at all because I mainly am sitting down writing, I'm getting a gut. And cutting toenails, for anyone who has a gut, creates a frothy and crimson apoplexy. Think of all the innards. In the sewer of this package that is the body. Beautiful machine, say the fantasists. And then you remember the package of shit that is your body. Of a heap of debris. Of the foulness of being alive. The intensity of wanting to be somebody. Brilliance, originality, conversation, car, horse, video, computer, certified checks, modernity, lovers, woman, ahhhhhh! I want to be ancient, the oldest possible even, crumbling to pieces and why not toothless? There are single teeth, bright ones, in tombs, in coffins. My hard gums can chew everything very well. There are scumbags ballsacks with all their teeth. And then I am not going to eat nuts or gnaw on bones (perhaps... gnawing on bones?... yes I can get to that). That toothless I am all wizened like an old woman's mouth? So what? What's wrong with being wrinkled up? Why would it be nicer to be smooth? Is the asshole beautiful? It is not. There was a girl, Adélia, who said that her asshole was beautiful. She probably didn't see anything beyond her beautiful little asshole. Assholes are putrid. Mine for example. Full of yellow hairs. And brownish, ignoble assholes. That disgusting Karl had a watercolor in his ample dining room: red brushstrokes on a black, frightened eye, gray folds. I was eating lobsters, looking at the watercolor and thought: and to think that everything will be torn apart by my ass. Meanwhile he, Karl, was going on about the beautiful, fragrant ring of his sister Cordélia. Bastard. He himself laughed as he downed oysters, squeezing lemons on them and trembling, he opened his mouth: there are women-cunts, there are women-cocks, there are women-dicks and there are women-oysters. Really? And how did that come to be? And a harangue arose about everything that was sucked and swallowed. I kept the lobsters in my stomach. After the picture of the father on the mahogany, ivory and mother-of-pearl dresser... the father a beauty yes, but what a deceptive smile! He must have dined on his son and daughter. Bermuda shorts, Prince racquets and that air of victory that he displayed in all the pictures. What a family! And your mother, how was she? He replied: this one's face. And he showed me a woman so beautiful that I almost fainted that night, puking in the lobster but thinking of her (I cannot stand contrasts). I, too, boy, would have slipped my nib in that mouth.

There are mothers who cannot be mothers. Succulent Madaleines. And isn't it that I am aroused and cannot state

Letters from a Seducer

the basics, the nontransferable of what I ought to say? To say that I am not here by chance on this beach, in this house, house yes, now there is no other name to define this oscillation of clay and straw, it is more than a ruin but not yet a home, it is a space only for someone to get aroused, think and live with Eulália. And incredibly it appears a space to reflect and grow dim... dim life's very vivid hues, dilute them in white satin, the color coming out of the cracked head of the other... this one here hard, already sated right now after having thought about the lady who looked like the mother of that nauseating Karl. Madame Grand, he said. And so it was. Grand Madame of my utopias! I want to get a little sleep. But I think it is not correct to have Eulália with the seafood and I like an ass here wondering whether I should or should not grab the coconuts and hearts of palm. But I see the pencil stub and how much I should gather up the coconuts for that. I stand. I put my hands on my waist, stretch my torso. There, on the face of the sea, a yacht passes. The rich and their theatricalities. Me and my tenement. My cramped being. My nobodies. Old films: I elegant, clean-shaven, fragrant, platinum cufflinks. Suddenly in the middle of the street I pulled them off and to the first person passing by: do you want them? The passerby's astonishment: I don't want them, sir, you think I'm a sucker? A lady is approaching, black hair, smooth, Chanel outfit: just a minute, ma'am... She stopped. There's a problem? No, ma'am, it's just that I made a promise to St. Thérèse of the Child Jesus... you familiar with her? Yes I know her, my mom has a special devotion to her. So it's the same with you as well... I repeat: I made a promise which is this: give away my platinum cufflinks if I could understand what I should do from here on out on

Earth, and just as you were passing, I understood. So I want to give you my platinum cufflinks because the promise was precisely that. What? she asks. To give away the cufflinks at the time that I had the *insight*. And I had it. And what is that? she asks, smiling. It's a kind of illumination, you know? More or less. No matter, ma'am, the fact is that I understand what I should do from now on. Take them. She opens her little hands and says What should I do with them? I don't know, ma'am, but perhaps maybe give them to your husband. I am divorced. Then your father. My father died two months ago. How did he die? It began to rain. Shall we have some coffee? It's that I was going to the dentist but... Do you have a lot of cavities? Why do you ask? Because then you can melt the cufflinks and lower your dentist bill. She alternates between looking at me and the cufflinks. Are you sure you want to give them to me? (I remember the series *Dallas*. Those characters so full of teeth horses women cufflinks.) Yes of course, I reply, and I got tired and wished her a good day. She paused. I started walking. She remained still, I looked back, she tucked them in her purse and yelled: they are beautiful! Thank you! Unbuttoned shirtsleeves. Mine. That was the beginning of the end. After the house the wife everything vanished. I went to a boarding house. That one. Ah, but I think that I still haven't spoken to you about the boarding house. Four in a room (it suggests degradation, but it isn't like that). A paratrooper who never appeared, always in the air, and when he appeared he was limping. Was it the jump? No, it was a tumble down the stairs. Another one, very much a psychopath. From time to time he would pull out his dick: I don't know what to do with it. Beat it, I said, and don't look at me like that. He worked in a hospital warehouse. And the nurses? I asked. Old women, sad, if only their being old did not matter because (he concluded) holes don't age but I cannot stand sad woman. At one point he asked me why I was writing without stopping and what I wrote.

I write bizarre things.

Bizarre is me having a cock and nothing happens with it.

there are other bizarre things.

name one.

I say: a necklace of anemones surrounds your face and in my eyes you definitely have earned a frame. He looks at me languidly... Yeah, that's lovely. And Valença and Resende who just arrived repeat together, in measured tones: a necklace of anemones surrounds your face and in my eyes you definitely have earned a frame... Right now I think there are other stupendously bizarre things to mention, think about, write down: black stones and thorns inside a bouquet of butterflies, some with punctured wings, glimmering, mauve, or a dovecote of screams...

how would that be?

friezes, strips, joyful bands, columbombastic screams.

And I should not stop. There is an orgy of phosphenes right and left, someone yells: listen! everything comes from the spirit! And pink lights, violet lights, clash in silver canes, gold comets over the cabinets, some opening and inside arabesques, letters, sounds from so many that fade, and a river of bizarreries finds a sea of languorous serpents, I read words between scales and waters... but silence! I should keep them, because they should be uttered only when my time comes. I repeat aloud: my time.

You want to know what time it is, sweetheart? It's late, I got all this stuff, My hand is hurt. Eulália. I kiss her small fingers, the nails bitten, tell her that without her life is a strange flower, perhaps a flower with only one petal.

that don't exist, Tiu

And I say to myself: meager, meager life.

Karl telling me: I would never put you in my texts. You are negligible, Tiu (and he's laughing), you are a semi-o(p)tic, look, and he put his right hand over his right eye and pretended to read a text, we look at you (he was looking at me), and it's as if we only saw your left side. And to think that that hyper-pretentious Karl goes around publishing books, has found editors! That pervert! That dandy. From time to time he would spout a phrase from Lawrence: "The penis is like a flagpole pointing to the stars"... He would choke with laughter. I look at my... Flagpole, star... yes I smile. Briefly. I'm sad, gentlemen. I'll tumble soon enough. Bent over, perhaps I should throw up. Vomit hopes, pains, the dish of blackberries, that *carré d'agneau* from Karl's dinner, vomit up all the fantasies about senhora Grand whoever she is, her Homerics tucked between taffetas and silks, thighs marked by my bites, the lipstick smeared across her mouth... I kissed her so many times that her lips grew bruised, the top and bottom ones, I licked her neck, tongue in her ears, her nostrils... lady of my utopias... and I alone in bed, my hand cupped, sweaty, getting into nothing.

Letters from a Seducer

look, a centipede, Tiu!

chilopod

what?

it's another name for a centipede

chilo... who?

Eulália is not real. She is right there in front of me but she isn't real. She moves and still does not exist. Maybe she has some materiality because I suspect I sometimes hear her speaking. Right now she is washing the seafood... and sings, "Crazy through the streets he walked and the poor thing was crying"... Now she stops singing: I told you, love, about Efizira who got bit on the head by a beach insect and ended up with all her hair standing on end? No. That's what happened. And then? Then Mr. Quietinho, her husband, almost died of shock, he thought that a spirit, Exu, was there inside her head... poor Efizira, the whole world running away from her, her hair sticking straight up... it was quite a commotion till they discovered that insect.

you think that here on this beach we got that insect, Tiu?

if you start to find yourself with your hair standing on end, it's because we got it.

Are you gonna be there writing for a long time, don't you wanna help me?

Me plummeting into an orange chaos. Redheaded brushstrokes within an orange chaos. *Bewusstsein. Bewusstsein*, is much more Awareness than consciousness. Consciousness is sibylline, languid, *Bewusstsein* is thick, hot. As is, in reality, consciousness. Being aware is *bewusstseinian*. Heavy, leaden, burning. I'm on fire. I am mortal and deep and conscious and yet I must stop at the broom's sweep, in a corner, like a rat. Not so, another tells me. It could even be in bed right up till then. Saying things. Henry James during a heart attack: "*So here it is at last, the distinguished thing.*" A fine thing. The ample woman in black that Marcel saw: "Celeste, leave the bedside lamp on, I want to see her better." And how will I see her? How will she present herself to me? Perhaps as senhora Grand. Sitting in the armchair, bosom covered in ribbons, blond hairdo, head raised to the right, eyes looking at no one, in her hand a letter... musical score or letter? The last one I wrote you: Beloved, Precious, come! regarding the *siddhis* and *samadis* that you want, you will have them with me. I will be your guide, your guru, your master. we will walk all those roads, dick behind you, plump, thick. you on all fours sometimes. kissing the dust of the blessed. Do you want that? I also know how to be holy. To flagellate myself. To flagellate you later. while I eat your cave I will flagellate your breasts, I will step away and flagellate your waist. afterwards I'll lick your entire body, you bleeding, gasping, beautiful. So it is true that you received the letter. Pleasured yourself later. Or did you fuck the painter? The female painter! But of course! Yes, that one: Elizabeth Vigée-Lebrun. I have to endure even that! That a woman would lick her pussy while she was soaking up my letter! Unbearable. Thus that look... unconscious, exhilarated, looking at no one. On second thought: the painter was painting and someone else was licking the bush. A man. Perhaps me even. And don't I remember? Of course, it was me. My black velvet pants, my

Letters from a Seducer

white silk shirt, long sleeves tight at the wrist. On my knees. While I licked Madame Grand, I masturbated. Elisabeth said: take a little more time, sir, don't make her cum, the rosy light coming from outside and this light on this view is everything I need, pause for a minute, ah, poor little thing, she stopped and that aquamarine left her eyes, resume, sir, and I there gasping beneath her skirts, what perfumes! raspberry and rosemary! she opens her fat thighs wider every time ahhhhh! she screamed. And I: fuck the painter, the rosy light, the aquamarine. We're sad once again.

what is it hmm, Tiu?

why?

you breathed deeply

it wasn't anything. it was someone here who fainted.

I'm kinda feeling like doing it, honey.

you are?

you gonna stop writing, no?

soon, Eulália.

read to me, go on, it is pretty? is the thing she does good for the spirit?

no, Eulália, it's a piggish thing.

hey, Tiu, didn't you say you were gonna stop with all that?

just a little longer, then I'll just talk about the bearded dick of God.

speak a little about that stuff of yours that's beautiful... speak of mine here... she puts her finger on it.

She lies down, I shuffle the papers, throw it all away, throw myself on top of Eulália, her pussy swallows my dick, now she sits on my waist, Eulália all stretched out, she's elegant when she fucks, I have told her, she has the air of a princess, and slowly rises and falls, a storm is coming, little clouds of sand cover the mat, the house-shack shakes, and she screams a thin and hard scream, a whip, a bone. Eulália kisses my eyes. As if I were dead. Not yet, the other tells me. And it's not going to be like this. How will it be? Someone holding my hands. Someone saying calm down, everything will pass, it is just a discomfort. And lights, landscapes before me: I a child, the dog next door, Pitt (someone back home liked an Englishman with that name), the sea and the sand crabs. Afterwards boarding school. Me climbing the stairs, my eye full of tears before the glass door. My mom and her silk *écharpes*—scarves. The goodbyes. Father Valentino: come on, come on and give your mother a smile. Goodbye, ma'am. Me at the chalkboard and then: senhor Stamatius, is the theorem finished? That's it, it is done. No, it's not done. And the fool Karl always bursting into laughter. Senhor Karl, come show senhor Stamatius how to prove a theorem. He and Father Kosta. Always the little secrets. Wasn't that creep already going into corners brushing his little ass against cassocks? He was quite handsome. Broad-shouldered, tall, with long eyelashes, blond hair. And isn't that cynical creep releasing a book? He is capable of anything. Of giving his asshole, penetrating the rim of some editor, sucking his cock until he makes it bleed, despicable weevil! he wanted it because he wanted to be a writer. He would ponder: Tiu, there's nothing like asceticism and abstraction. A writer isn't a saint, my man. The thing is inventing ballsy stuff, things to turn people on, pussies in hand, the guys want to read something that makes them forget they're mortal and shit. He continues: Tiu, with your mania for infinitude who is going to read you? I bet I will be the first in the window and you there in the bookstore's confines. Which is it, my man? Give some moquettes to the fat woman in black, turn off the bedside lamp, read lowbrow texts, or other people's texts to her, mine for example, sit on pointy knees, tear death to pieces, shatter her clit, milkily utter some sodden expletives, she will smile, will be full of humor and saliva, she will think it beautiful to call you Stamatius, your Greek name, and she will say: you are pure life, I am going to give you a long time. Women are starving for caresses, and few people diddle the Damned One. Do you understand?

Eulália: you wanna eat pasta with marjoram and a plate of seafood?

where did you get pasta?

oh, baby, I shed a tear for the Ox Bar owner. Only one tear, baby.

I was betrayed, I thought. But still. To whom will I extend my hands when the lady arrives? Will there be light in the room? Dazzling light or shade? Will I still have time to become perfect, perhaps a saint? And if I cut off the sea bream or bludgeon it so as never to get hard again? Or if I cover my nostrils with tiny mat threads so that I will never again smell the scent of camellias or bearded oysters or my own scent which emerges from life and as a result from fear? And why do I continue to sully papers trying to project my breath, my sounds, into the body of words? What words should I say to

Madame when she arrives? And what if it is not a woman and is a boy? Somewhat slender, sorrowful, mannered... Death: a sad, thin sissy. So I cannot cut off the sea bream before training it so that it becomes skilled at adjusting from something sweet to a flimsy little butthole. And what if the hole is deep? There are shitholes as long as tunnels... To eat death's fig... But will that keep me alive? I'm lying there, gasping, extending my hands and still have to get up to fuck the skinny kid, there in the corner?

good evening, dona Eulália, senhor Pedro of Ox Bar sent me to deliver this can of sauce for your pasta dish.

oh young man, thanks a lot, I really needed it.

Drenched with fright, I'm the one who repeats without stopping thank you thank you my God, it's only a skinny kid delivering a can of sauce for the pasta dish.

your eyes are bugging out, Tiu, you scared?

I tell her that the tear she shed for senhor Pedro at Ox Bar was as good as if the teary eye were a finger.

what you saying, honey?

that you probably fingered the shlong of that guy for him to have shown such kindness.

She becomes sad. She says she will not put the sauce on my pasta, that I am going to eat it very plain, without anything. I smile. I give her a kiss on the bellybutton. And while she cooks I will go for a walk on the beach. It's no longer raining. It's a crescent moon. I stretch my arms, do genuflections, place my hands on my hips, puff up my chest and breathe

Letters from a Seducer

deeply. I feel sick. I cannot inhale life so deeply. I sit. There is nothing on the sea. No light. No vessel. Lights once again in my left eye. How did the guy put it? Phosphenes. That's it. I calm myself down. They are just phosphenes. A shard of red-lacquer is more insistent. I like that red. I had a Chinese lacquer box once. I kept tie pins and platinum cufflinks in it. It was a beautiful box. I bought it on the Via Veneto. When I was that other one. The one of the cufflinks. When I was a friend of Karl. When I played polo. When I was rich. When I still thought there would be enough time to write, that when I was older, yes, I would write... And the futility flooded my flesh, my bones, full of futility I made a blague: *Bewusstsein*? It sounds vulgar and grimy. Then the *Bewusstsein* grew and no longer provided me a respite. Consciousness of being here on Earth, and not having been holy or sufficiently a bastard. To invent, to save myself. To cheat death claiming that this isn't me, that she got the wrong address, the postman pissed his pants when he saw the dog and hollered: but this is not senhor Stamatius's dog, nor senhor Karl's, so this warning with a black target has to be just for the one who has the dog, but how can I hand over the warning if there's this dog here in the door? That confusion. And with that I am gaining time. The big dog here licking my face. It should be the dog of the Ox Bar man. That one who farted. Not the man, nor the dog. The ox. I pity oxen cows dogs. Animals. Creatures also. All of us. I am all piety. I pity my dick also. I always ought to talk about my dick. Or about the nuts. Or the member. It's what the publisher wants. "You can ruminate a little, big man, but always get around to the screwing." I am worried because beyond the 1,500 positions in the *Kama Sutra* I'm supposed to create new ones. And new approaches. I'm even sweating. I called some friends here onto the beach so that they can tell me some smut. Boring bores. That he fucked a goose. Croc croc, fine. The other: that he licked a frog's skin because he got high, and while he was licking (I thought he was fucking the toad?) he put his cock in his girl's asshole. And the frog on her back, more exactly on the nape of her neck, wanting to jump to the puddle stoned. I say no, these stories won't work, they have to have real whorishness. Then they want explanations, concise data, but more towards the piggish or more subtle? But more filthy or more sensual? On the grotesque side? Eh, eh, eh, my man, there isn't much new. Cum in the ear? I did that one day and my wife got sick, she had to have the otolaryngologist clean her out. Whoa! And the otolaryngologist said: ma'am, there are basically three holes made for what the lady allowed to be done in her ear and there is no need to cite the three, but ears and nostrils are unfit to receive semen, do you understand? You will come down with otitis and sinusitis, and you want to know what else? you're a sow. He slammed the door in her face. And then? From that day until now that cum has not come out of there. I said to my wife: but that cum in your ear hole, I've never heard it said that anyone had that big a hole. And then? Then I made my wife lie on her side, on my knees, the soaked ear on the other side, and while she was sucking me I gave her three or four slaps on the top till a little of all of that dripped onto the floor. What a disgusting story! And that won't do for you? Of course not, man. OK, so you don't want either gross or subtle. And subtle would be? Is it licking the swallow's rose? And fornicating with a daisy? Look, people, nobody understood anything. Let's go back to

Letters from a Seducer

my hut to eat seafood and noodles. Where's Eulália? Tired of waiting for me, she ate alone. She went to sleep. I strike my friends from my memory. I stand there in the middle of the hut, looking around. And in a corner I see the devil, filthy. He is naked. A little sad. His dick shriveled up. I say M'Bata, a magic formula for him to disappear. He says: don't be silly, do you like Blake? Very much, but please go away. Listen to these verses: "Let each choose one habitation: / His ancient infinite mansion: / One command, one joy, one desire, / One curse, one weight, one measure / One King, one God, one Law." Beautiful yes, I think, mansions and kings, order pleasure, and it's another who got the address wrong. Where's the dog? It is with you Stamatius or Karl or Cordélia or senhora Grand or Madame Lamballe, let me correct that, Princess, okay then princess, what are you writing? Who is that with the keening face? You think Eulália has a keening face? *Undoubtedly.* You materialized your howl about life and it's so poignant it was born a woman. And it was born as you wanted to be: poor in spirit. And as you see yourself: a crystalline sensuality. And a touch of pity, a touch of debauchery, and delicacy in sex because deep down you fear that everything degenerates into death.

why is your dick so shriveled up?

disuse, my dear.

you don't say, I always associated you with quivering cocks.

no. That is God and Lawrence. D. H. Not the other.

do you like him, Lawrence?

I really like his Reflections on the Death of a Porcupine.

and the rest?

very naive, almost a child.

is he really? do you have contact with him?

sometimes he despairs because where he is he has no one to talk to.

where is that?

the recess hour in "The Blue Angel"

what is that?

the name of the school. it is where all those with good intentions go.

seems boring.

Peaceful, big man. Well, I'm going. Wake your double there and give her a lay soon. That will undo your bad impression of my presence. I was honest with you. I showed up just as I am: nude. With a shriveled dick. But I can appear with His gourd. I terrify the arrogant. I shove my turnip in them. They become fanatics. They think they are conversing with God, the poor things, feeling all that fire in their hole.

Eulália wakes up screaming: I dreamed of the horned beast, Tiu! come here, see, it's warm in here, what are you doing standing there? come closer, come on, put it in here, in my petunia.

what do you know about petunia?

at the carnival, Tiu, did you not hear the man talking about the scent of petunias?

Letters from a Seducer

where was that?

when I went to my cousin's house because you were only writing, she had a television that Saturday, and the man was talking only about petunias and another who was filming the girl showed only the girl's backside and box, we didn't see the face, only the lower parts... could it be that the man that was filming the girl was a dwarf, Tiu? so petunia must be the people's little thing... when the thing appeared he was saying look at the petunia, people!

petunia is a flower, Eulália.

what's it like?

like your funk.

what's a funk?

it's a petunia.

I open her legs and put my finger in the funk in the petunia in the cherry in the cunny, she opens up, I get hard, and while I meddle in her midsection the certainty comes to me that it was the Dark One the creator of this chaos that is man, this disorder that only knows how to feel, only feeling is what can be learned, only feeling is what has knowledge palpates kneads opens rips.

ouch, Tiu, you're hurting me.

So I come out of her mid-parts, out of the warmth, and in the middle of the hut with my dick hard I start screaming: I am God! I am God! Eulália laughs: well, it's true, God must be just like this. I say: it really is true, Eulália, it's exactly like this. Who told you this, Tiu? The demon. Eulália closes herself up: I'm afraid. I return to the bed, take her in my arms, caress her pubes and discourse on the Dark One, his being totally nude, his shriveled dick, his sadness. She starts laughing very slowly, says that she always thought the horned one had a huge one. So that's what he explained to me tonight, that it isn't, and I saw, Eulália, that it's so tiny, a wrinkled little thing. Pitiful, no? And he also told me that you don't exist, Eulália, that you are my invention. It may be, sweetheart, she responds, I like you so much that if one day you stop loving me, I will turn into a speck, tiny leaf, crab.

why a crab?

ah... because a crab's so sad.

I think: I really did construct my squealing-woman-in-life in a poignant and delicate, submissive and patient way.

I'm swallowing Eulália. I'm resigning. I'm becoming more and more alone. My bones will remain. Should I polish my bones before vanishing?

Letters from a Seducer

NEW CANNIBALISMS

I

I BEGAN TASTING HER FINGERS. They were expressive, forceful. How often her blunt index finger had brushed against my face! She continually repeated her "you see" rather coldly and impersonally. I am a Doctor of Letters. She called herself an autodidact.

autodidact?!?!

autodidact of life, ignoramus, wretch, she growled.

I put up with her for several years. I married her *à cause de* that hole buried deep in her creamy buttocks. After I shoved my stick in it I smiled warmly and for a long time. Then I was sad. I sensed I had made a huge mistake. But every night with "you see" or not, I gave her the bone. Between the gaiety and the weeping I kept on putting up with her grimaces, her sinister domesticity. One night, during dinner, my steak escaped my plate. She began her "you sees" and notions about table etiquette. I listened attentively and up to a point with real, intimate ceremony, just as if listening to a Nobel Laureate's speech on the day of the award presentation. Then, maintaining my cool inside and out, I made the first careful gesture: to get the steak. Its trajectory had ended beneath the stairwell. She started laughing hysterically and repeating "you see you see," you are a perfect imbecile, a buffoon, an idiot. I grabbed the steak and put it back on the dish. I wiped the dust from my knees. The floor was filthy. She never cleaned under the stairs. Soon after that I issued a huge roar, like a large animal, and in a Nureyev leap, with great precision, buried the knife in her bosom. She stood there, still smiling, crystallized. At that exact moment, I cut off her index finger, I point it at her selfsame face and repeat: "You see, ma'am, what an autodidacticism of life leads to." I clean her fingernail which was always the one poking me in the ass. Yes, I liked it. Her I don't know. Now, befouled with hate, I hurl the finger out the window. The night is cold and there are stars out. It is acts like this, you see, that make this life what it is: sordid and immutable.

II

WE HAD ENDLESS DISCUSSIONS. I showed him my texts and he said: you have no breathing room, buddy, everything ends too quickly, you do not develop the character, the character wanders around, has no density, is not real. But that's all I mean, I do not want contours, I do not want density, I want the guy lightly-drawn, concise, rushed for its own sake, free of personal data, the guy floating, yes, but he is alive, more alive than if he were trapped by words, by acts, he floats free, you understand? No. And he straightened his glasses, no and no. I found it convenient not to show him any more texts. He found me and insisted: hof hof hof, breathing room, buddy, breathing room, shoo away the little fluctuating clouds, give body to your carcasses, sink their feet in the soil. I implored: stop that, stop it, one day perhaps you'll understand. He did not understand. In front of friends, my wife, my children he started in: hof hof hof, breathing room, buddy. One day we went to the beach. Between one caipirinha and another I proposed that we swim to the island. He weakly said yes, but agreed. In the middle of the crossing, while he was drowning, I perfected my *butterfly*, and my pace was swift, harmonious, quite vigorous. I shouted to him before seeing him disappear: this is breathing room, motherfucker. I am at peace. And to him I dedicate this, my brief text, light, concise, rushed for its own sake, free of personal data, much more alive than he is dead.

III

THE MAN COMPLAINED: I already said that I don't like seeing you wearing those sheer blouses.

why?

because your nipples are visible.

so what? nipples are beautiful, dear.

Yes, women's nipples are beautiful, petite pink ones, like coins, she petite and fair all over, a little Dutch madonna... have you ever seen a little Dutch madonna? Certainly, all those Vans painted little Dutch madonnas. Without clogs.

I know the nipple is beautiful, but I don't want everyone seeing yours.

The woman was sweet, graceful. Graceful is also pretty. He looked at her and thought: why is it that tiny women have so much luck with men? Some of his friends had also fallen for tiny women. They seemed like childhood pets (when one had a childhood), those cuddly little things, cubs puppies bunnies, those we slept with as little people, we held tight in our arms, between our thighs... little women-children, little women-creatures.

She: no one cares about the nipples, honey, plus these sheer blouses are so refreshing...

The mania for self-display that women have: at the last carnival he was completely stunned. The entire time asses, pussies, wild shaking, spasms. The time will come when asses and pussies should manifest other qualities beyond the obvious ones, because self-exhibition grows boring. For example there might be talking asses, pussies that metamorphose into flowers, behinds that whistle Mozart, who knows. He met that petite woman at that carnival. Her nipples out. Okay, it was carnival. But unacceptably, every day now, his wife and her nipples through the streets. He insisted: cover the nipples. She became offended, peevish, would not talk any more.

One night he thought again about his own history, his, the loneliness, and sorrowfully, sweetly, he acquiesced.

okay, put on the blouse you want, let's take a walk.

Shimmering, sheer, her blouse showed not only the nipples, but both teats, firm extremely round quivering. She asked for beer. He asked for ice cream. The men at the bar looked at the petite woman like he was not there. She laughed: I'm pretty, no? It was then he bewilderingly growled:

you're going to be beautiful now. In a flash he grabbed her teats, bit her left nipple, sliced off the little strawberry areola and slathered in blood amidst the screams he placed the nipple atop the ice cream, marshmallow and banana. He yelled: now, sweetheart, everyone can see, suck and gorge on your nipple, goodbye. The ambulance arrived soon after. The guys in the bar explained: it's that one there, with the sheer blouse. No one knew what finally became of the nipple. The name of the bar changed: Nipple Bar. There are new ice cream flavors. A strawberry on the top. Ice cream, lady? With nipple or without nipple, ma'am?

Letters from a Seducer

IV

TRULY. HE WAS SURE NOW. The girl was following him. Checkered mini-skirt, white blouse, knee socks, a tiny tie. Was she eleven twelve years old? He walked three blocks slowly listening to those small steps behind him. Patent leather shoes. Minimal hop. He stopped at the window of a cigar shop. English Swedish Swiss pipes. If she stopped at that window everything would be clear: the girl was following him. She stopped. Do you like the pipes? he asked. Do you like being sucked? she asked in response. He blushed. By grown women yes, he answered. And what am I? A child. Someone stopped beside them and they grew silent. She took his hand: so, Dad, would you like this one? The one beside them left. She continued: look at me, stand very close, I am going to suck my finger the way I will suck your dick. He looked all around him. Don't be silly, no one is looking, and she began to stick her thumb in her mouth, rolling it around and licking it from root to tip.

but my dick is not your thumb. It's bigger.

but I have a large arcade.

what??!

My dentist says I have a pretty large arcade.

She takes my hand again, says let's go for a walk, and points to a little plaza where there are benches and ice cream carts and popcorn. We sit.

why are you doing this?

because I want some money.

ahh.

I like clothes and money buys clothes.

but I can buy you clothes without you sucking me off.

no, I like to do my duty.

ah, you mean that you would not accept it if I gave you the clothes without you sucking me off...

yep, never that, I like to work.

I observed her dark little face, her big eyes, her sharp nose, her somewhat narrow upper lip, the lower lip fleshy, scarlet. Would you like some ice cream? No. Look, girl, I've got nowhere to take you. But I will suck you right here. Here?!?! Sure. You take off your jacket, I lay my head on your lap, you cover me with your jacket like I was asleep, you buy a newspaper over there, and while you pretend to read I will take your dick out slowly and I'll also be sucking slowly. Only you pay me before. That was enough. I said okay. I went over, bought the paper, took off my jacket, gave her the money and she did everything and more than promised. Two years later, I never again came with any woman. And I retrace the same path and crazily strike that bench and buy a paper but I never ran into her again. A friend told me: dream, stress, drunk, powder, that's what it was, man. I said no. And my dick knows that.

V

HE WOULD LIKE TO BE COHERENT, calm, frivolous. Yes, because there is cohesion and calmness in frivolity. Or do you not think so? Then think about it again. He had a horror of sex. Smells slime gymnastics convulsion. Principally horror at the silence of those hours. Better, horror of squeals and other sounds that seemed like sounds from the depths, from wells, from bubbles. He liked to sit and read. Principally Chesterton and his *Orthodoxy*. Friends would ask him: you don't like to fuck, right? No, he answered, it disgusts me. Disgusted by what? The bodies joining, the smells, the noise. He was left alone with his books and his disgust. He liked to think but little by little he was smelling the scent of ideas, and the most powerful ones, the most genuine ones, the most vehement ones had the same smell as sex and of that casuarine slime. So by discipline and fasting he was emptying his mind. He saw colors and the colors did not have smells and that was good. He sat down on the floor of the living room and stayed there until he noticed that he had turned into a living point of golden light. Until the young guy woke him and said: want some more junk in the trunk, doc?

VI

I WAS 18 YEARS OLD, she 29, a seamstress, and she came every Thursday to redo the embroidery of Mom's bed linens, Madeira Island sheets, beautiful beautiful ones, but the embroidery coming apart here and there. Her name was Antonia, daughter of Portuguese, slender, gentle, her mouth delicate, her teeth tiny. I came home from cram school at 4 pm, panting, climbed the hill in a race, afraid of missing her because she would leave the house at 5 pm. I was in love. One day I could not stand it: Antonia, I don't know if it will upset you, but I love you. Your mother will only be back by 6, she asked me to wait for her, and she went shopping. Her voice was icy. Strictly formal. I blushed and believed I had offended her. I apologized and went up the stairs, head down, towards my room. In the middle of the stairs I turned to see her perhaps for the last time. Antonia was sitting, legs opens, the blue-torquoise skirt rolled up to her waist. Stupefied, I almost did not believe what I saw, but then I recovered and descended the stairs slowly and opened my fly. I sat on her thighs, I just like open scissors, but before penetrating her, I came. She smiled, showing her little teeth, and made me kneel before her. The thing was there. There were no panties. She covered us with one of Mom's magnificent sheets. She seated. I kneeling. Before starting to suck her I made the sign of the cross, asking God to pass my first test. I went at it. She came many times, and in coming repeated Oh Jesus, Oh Jesus. We were decidedly Catholic. For two weeks I lived the most dazzling Thursdays, because Mom decided

Thursday would be a good day to shop and approved Antonia's presence looking after the house until 6. Mom did not like me staying all by myself in the old mansion. Previously it had been a posh neighborhood, later infested with whorehouses and thieves. One day, as if through the demonic arts as the bishop would say, Mom arrived at 5:30. And there we both were, under one of the magnificent sheets, Antonia with legs open and I with dick still hard, big tongue out. It was horrible. Fainting, vomiting, Mom's convulsions. Until today (years went by), I can only gain pleasure kneeling before the box, making the sign of the cross and asking my partner to repeat Oh Jesus, Oh Jesus several times. And there's also the sheet. Indispensible, but it need not be from Madeira Island. Thank God. Otherwise I would have to move to another country because I do not know anyone who still has sheets from that island, and mother in a rage donated ours to Ms. Blond, owner of a famous whorehouse ten blocks away. I never saw Antonia again. But she, now 39, must still be beautiful, so fragrant her pussy and thighs and seated somewhere with her splendid legs open and so intense in her lyrical and very modest Oh Jesus.

VII

I WILL NEVER FORGET that providential prolonged and silent fart of age 14. I was crazy about Nena, a creole virgin but big-bottomed and voracious, who liked to bite my slit while I diddled her middle amidst the clumps of grass. At noon on a Sunday, after filling my belly with beans, turnips jerky and pumpkin, I met horny Nena waiting for me in the bush.

I'm feeling it right now, she said.

feeling what?

like giving you some nookie.

right now?

and what's wrong with now?

well, because people die if they bang after stuffing their gut.

what idiocy, stupid, the entire world would be dead if they thought like you.

She was leaning closer, sucking me and biting my mouth, her tongue sliding along the mucous membrane, she pulled my basket out of my pants and while she was massaging my acorns with her left hand, with her right hand she was trying a to and fro with my gourd. She whispered, "come on inside the tunnel, come on." I thought—I'm going to die now, at age 14, without saying goodbye to father to mother to grandmother, the sun beaming on my crown. I screamed without screaming, a pained cry, a plea in the back of the chest: save me Saint Expeditus, patron saint of the impossible, give me a sign that I will not die if I put it in Nena now. And when I went to stick

Letters from a Seducer

it in, out of me came that long silent round hot fat stewed living fart. Nena paused her caressing finger. She looked me hard in the eye:

you farted, Nico?

I uh... I didn't fart.

if you didn't fart, you're already dead.

She gave me a slap in the face, said that was disrespectful and she left. I lay down on the grass, remained stretched out there looking at the sky: thanks for the sign, Saint Expeditus, thanks so much, better fart than die. The following day I wanted to tell Nena about the sign but she fled my grasp, muttering: "No, I don't feel like banging people who fart." She must have gone from man to man throughout her life because at some point or other even doctors ministers ambassadors or kings, if they have an asshole, fart.

what a disgusting thing, Tiu.

why Eulália?

cause nobody likes to talk about these things.

but look, Eulália, if everyone were to remember what comes out of their butt, everyone would be more generous, show more solidarity, more...

what's solidarity, baby?

it's not being as solitary as this.

ain't I here?

Then I farted. And Eulália got up just like Nena, and because of that fart very quickly moved away from there.

VIII

FOR TEN YEARS NOW HE HAS BEEN TRYING to write the first verse of a poem. He was a perfectionist. At 30, the day before yesterday morning, he shouted to his wife: I got it, Jandira! I got it!

She (sitting in bed disheveled)	What? The job?
He	The verse of course, silly, look at the shine in my eye, look!
She (yawning)	Let me hear it, baby.

He slowly recited the first verse: "Like the fruit fitted to your round..." Jandira interrupting: Huh... round? But not all fruit is round...

He	They're metaphors, love
She	Metaphors?!?!
He	Yes... And there are also anacoluthons, zeugmas, aphereses.
She	?!?!? But where does the banana fit in here?

He hanged himself very early in the morning from a mango tree. The message attached to his chest said: the mango is not round, the papaya also is not, the jackfruit much less so. and you are an idiot, Jandira. Bye.

She (a little sad after reading the note) And the pear, sweetie? And the pear, which nobody knows what it is? And the starfruit!! And the starfruit, love!

HE WAS TELLURIC AND UNIQUE. He was dreaming. He dreamt of goodbyes and shadows. He dreamt of gods. He was cruel because he had always been desperate. He encountered a human-angel. So that they might live together, on Earth, forever, he cut off his wings. The other killed himself, plunging into the waters. I am still alive today. I'm old. At night I drink a lot and look at the stars. Often, I write. Then I reconsider that one, the snowy breath, the desperation. I lie down. Austerely, I dream that I sow black beans and wings across a dark, sometimes mother-of-pearl, earth.

END

AVAILABLE AND COMING SOON FROM PUSHKIN PRESS CLASSICS

The Pushkin Press Classics list brings you timeless storytelling by icons of literature. These titles represent the best of fiction and non-fiction, hand-picked from around the globe – from Russia to Japan, France to the Americas – boasting fresh selections, new translations and stylishly designed covers. Featuring some of the most widely acclaimed authors from across the ages, as well as compelling contemporary writers, these are the world's best stories – to be read and read again.

MURDER IN THE AGE OF ENLIGHTENMENT
RYŪNOSUKE AKUTAGAWA

THE BEAUTIES
ANTON CHEKHOV

LAND OF SMOKE
SARA GALLARDO

THE SPECTRE OF ALEXANDER WOLF
GAITO GAZDANOV

CLOUDS OVER PARIS
FELIX HARTLAUB

THE UNHAPPINESS OF BEING A SINGLE MAN
FRANZ KAFKA